Very

By Da̶̶̶̶̶r

Copyright © 2012 by David Spiller

All rights reserved. No part of this book may be reproduced in any form on by an electronic or mechanical means, including information storage and retrieval systems, without permission in writing from the publisher, except by a reviewer who may quote brief passages in a review.

Also by David Spiller:

Pilot Error

Out of Burma

Great Singers of the 20th Century

Bridger's Diary – a Mozart fantasy

Girl at Dunkirk

(Available on Amazon)

~ Tracey ~

Tracey went down the High Street with Catrina after school. She looked across at her friend's skinny frame, and up (several inches up) at the black face and green hair. The last thing she'd ever expected was going about with a West Indian girl, but Catrina was one of the few who stood up to her. Anyway, Kat made her laugh. She was loyal too.

'Fancy comin' round the Bricklayers later on,' Kat said. 'Me bruvver's payin'. It's 'is birthday.'

'Sorry Kat, I can't. Got somefin' on.'

'Wot's that, then?'

'Can't tell yer.'

Kat, who knew the most intimate details of Tracey's life, gave her friend the slow stare. 'Wos up, Trace?'

'Tell yer tomorrer, promise. It's best you don't know, believe me.'

'All right.'

Kat brushed an affectionate hand across the back of Tracey's neck as they walked on. No fuss. It was one of the things Tracey liked about her friend. They had disagreements but not tantrums. Who needed them?

They went on past the betting shop and the launderette, the DVD store, the legal aid office, two closed and shuttered shop fronts adorned with graffiti. They passed the greengrocer's with its row of yams in the window, and Tracey said she could never eat stuff like that and Kat said her mum did them twice a week. At the hairdressing place they waved through the window at Cheryl, who'd left school the previous year and was bent over a client. A scrawled note cellotaped to the window said there was a vacancy on the staff for a trainee.

'Nuvver three months an' I'd be goin' for that,' Kat observed.

'Not if I got there first,' said Tracey.

'Go on, Trace!' Kat feigned amazement. 'You not goin' on to uni, then?'

Tracey stopped on the pavement, hands on hips. Unlike Kat she rarely laughed, but the unusual glittering expression that sometimes crossed her pale features had to serve instead. 'Well I might, of course. We 'eard about some bloke called Wordsworf in English today. 'E 'ad a bastard kid, 'is sister was mental and 'is friend was a drug addict. I thought "I could do somefin' wiv this".'

A bike pulled up at the kerbside. The youth astride it wore a fake leather jacket with the words 'I'm a sex maniac' emblazoned across the back. He scattered his sentiments freely amongst the evening shoppers along the pavement.

'Ere, Tracey, I really fancy you. Will you come out wiv me?'

Tracey turned in genuine amazement. 'You wot?'

'No, I mean it, Trace.'

She took a few steps towards him, head bent in thought. 'Two fings about that Kevin. Try an' imagine that you an' me 'ave bin shipwrecked on a desert island. There's just the two of us there - nuffink else except sand and rocks an' stuff - and then you find a pineapple, and you ask me to share it wiv you.'

'Yeah?' Kevin looked puzzled but attentive.

'Well, what I'd do is I'd go to the other end of the island, as far away from you as possible, I'd climb a tree and then I'd eat some poison berries. Does that answer your question about goin' out wiv you?'

Kat laughed, but Kevin gamely got up off the canvas for more.

'And the other fing?'

'Wot?'

'You said there was two fings.'

'Oh yes, thank you for remindin' me. Wot is the point in askin' me out, dumbo, when you know very well that I'm already goin' out wiv Barry?'

Kevin did his 'I'm amazed' look. 'You 'aving' a laugh?'

'Sorry?'

'Barry! Barry's gay, ain't'e?'

Tracey was no taller than five-three in ankle socks, but her body was compact and - used as a human cannon-ball - could do some damage. It struck Kevin just after her fists, and sent him and bike crashing into the road. Her knee found his groin the moment before Kat pulled her clear.

'That's enough, Trace. Look, you've gone and got oil on your jeans.'

'Oh, bugger.'

''E's not worth that, is 'e? Come on.'

'I s'pose.'

''E's not.'

''Ere,' cried Kevin, tangled with his bike on the ground, but he was already past news. They continued on down the pavement as if nothing had happened.

'Well.' Kat gave her cheeky grin. 'It's nice to know your Barry gets you goin' anyway.'

'Leave it out, Kat. My dog's got a bigger dick than 'im.'

Kat chortled. 'Still...you like 'im. 'E turns you on.'

'I like 'im all right,' Tracey said, after considering this, 'When 'e's not being a pain in the bum. And the most careless little bugger you ever saw...'

'Careless!'

'Forget that, Kat. Forget I spoke. 'E don't turn me on though. Don't get that idea. I mean, 'e don't know nuffing.'

'Oh, that. Yeah, I know what you mean.' Kat's expression was all sympathy. 'Same fing wiv Wayne.'

'I mean, 'ow can they, Kat? We don't know nuffing. When you're 15 you can't 'ardly do yer bra up. It's all ahead of us. I 'ope so, anyway.'

They stopped on their usual corner, where Kat went one way, Tracey the other. Kat shrugged. 'What to do?'

'There's ways round it.'

'What are they, then?'

It was on the tip of her tongue to say something, but Tracey restrained herself. 'Finkin' of becomin' a nun, ain't I. 'Ave ter go now. See yer, then.'

'Yeah. See yer.'

*** *** ***

Just after 7.30 Tracey descended the stairs at home, moving quietly. Gone were the jeans and knitted top. She wore two-inch heels, a blouse, and a skirt. A skirt! And she'd spent 20 minutes on her make-up. She'd got a hand on the front door when her father appeared in the hall.

'Tracey.' He looked her over. 'What's all this?'

'It's a birthday do in the pub. Kat's bruvver.'

'You know what I mean. Why this get-up? Why the skirt?'

'I'm makin' an effort, dad, like you always say. Don't you like it?'

Another inspection. 'Hmm. You look very nice.'

'Thanks.'

'The pub, you say. You mean the Bricklayers?'

'Yeah.'

'You know what I'm going to say. Ten-thirty at the latest.'

'Of course, dad. Ten-thirty.'

'The latest, mind you. Have a good time then.'

She walked 200 yards to the High Street - the shoes pinching her feet - stood at the bus stop a while, then boarded a number 34. It carried her five miles north to a smarter area. Alighting, she asked the way to the posh hotel that she knew lay close by, and walked there too. Being unfit, she felt quite puffed by the time the heels took her through the hotel swing doors towards an imposing reception desk.

He was there as he'd said, wearing a dark suit and carrying a copy of The Daily mail, which was their signal. She stopped, pretending to straighten her skirt, and took in the details. Now was the moment - one of them, anyway - to turn on those heels and disappear. But no, he looked tolerable enough. About forty. Medium height. Filled out, but not fat. A reasonable enough face; not greasy, or shifty. A lot of 'nots', she thought to herself - but that was the best you could manage in this game.

She knew he'd be inspecting her in the same way, and that he could also turn tail. But she approached slowly and, as they'd agreed, said 'Hello dad', leaning up so he could stoop to kiss her cheek in full view of the reception staff.

'Shall we go on into the restaurant?' he said.

Sitting about in that chilly room was the worst bit, she reckoned. The white-clothed tables stretched away in antiseptic rows. Why did people do it? A waitress approached and asked about drinks. Tony - that was the name he'd given - had told her to have something 'non-alcoholic', and Tracey ordered an orange juice she didn't want.

'So.' His eyes gave her a good going over. 'You came.'

'An' you did an' all.'

'Of course I did.'

'Well you would do, wouldn't you,' Tracey told him. 'You get to climb all over some innocent young girl for nothin'. A man like you would come. Course you would.'

'What do you mean - a man like me?'

'Are you married?'

'Certainly not,' he said, but the little hesitation suggested otherwise. She was good at knowing when people were lying.

'You all say that.' She hadn't planned to needle him, but it was her style. The words just came out.

'Have you done this before then?'

'You fink you're the first?'

'Have you?'

'Yeah.'

'How many times?'

'Look, that's enough questions. I done it wiv one bloke, orl right?'

He shushed her as the waitress brought the drinks, and they sat in uneasy silence while glasses were laid on the table.

'So you liked it enough to try it again,' he said, when the waitress had gone.

'It was OK, yeah. I'd 'ave done it wiv 'im again.'

'Why didn't you?'

''E didn't ask me, did 'e.'

'I wonder why.'

'It's none of your business.'

'I think I can guess.' 'Tony' had lowered his voice, and was staring into her eyes. 'You've done yourself up very nicely, Tracey. You look great, actually. But you don't look sixteen, which is what you told me you were. And when you were with this other man you'd have been even younger. My guess is he got the wind up. He'd have gone to gaol if it got out.'

'But it didn't get out.'

He sat there looking, and she knew he was weighing up the risk. As for Tracey, she'd already made up her mind. She decided the moment she saw him. It was her way. Not that she liked the bloke especially, but liking didn't come into it. He wasn't stupid. He wasn't disgusting. There she went again, listing the 'wasn'ts'. In fact he was much as she'd expected from long chats on the Internet, and then that conversation in the call box that she'd insisted on. He'd do for her purpose. The pressure in Tracey's groin told her so. As long as he had the bottle for it.

'How old are you?' he said.

'I told you. I'm sixteen.'

'I'm sorry, Tracey, I don't believe you.'

'Well I 'aven't brought me birth certificate, 'ave I.'

Still the man sat undecided. 'We'll eat, and see how it goes,' he said.

'Not bloody likely.' Now was the moment to pressurise. 'I can't eat in 'ere. I'll puke.' She saw the waitress moving towards them. 'She's comin' to take our order. Tell 'er I'm ill. Tell 'er anyfink.'

'And then what?'

'You know what. Take me to your room and fuck me.'

It seemed like an age before the girl reached the table. 'I'm sorry,' Tony told her, 'We won't be staying.' He gave the waitress a weary shrug. 'My daughter's not feeling too good. You know how it is. We'll have to leave.'

'I'm sorry to hear that, sir.'

***   ***   ***

At 4am Tracey left the hotel. Not that the encounter was a disaster, but she'd had enough. She waited till Tony went to the toilet, then slipped from the room clutching her clothes. She heard him blundering out after her, calling 'Tracey' in a hoarse whisper. She had to dress on the staircase, with Tony just beyond the fire doors. Her feet felt cold on the tiled floor. She lingered there till he gave up, then plunged down the stairs. In reception the night porter gave an odd look, but said nothing.

The sudden departure was unplanned, and bus services had long been discontinued. She had no money for taxis, so it had to be Shank's pony. 'The most boring two hours of me whole bloomin' life,' she told Kat afterwards. Had she ever walked five miles before?; Tracey didn't think so. Once she'd left the shops behind, the endless main road ('dead straight' Tracey moaned) seemed indistinguishable, one bit from the next; row on row of drab suburban houses. After half a mile she took off the heels and walked on bare feet. An hour in it started to drizzle. On she went with that pugnacious short stride, feet slightly splayed, chin set. She wasn't sorry to have gone - Tracey didn't do regret - but she bloody well wanted to be home in her own bed.

It was nearly 6am when she slipped quietly through the front door and into the kitchen to make herself a cup of tea. No lights were on, so finding her father there was a shock. He was at the kitchen table, head in hands. As she shambled in his head came slowly up. It struck Tracey then that she never properly looked at her father, not really. He was just there at home, a fixture. This time, though, she did see him. Her father's hair had fallen over his eyes, which were blinking from lack of sleep, but she saw his expression and knew she'd been the cause of it. What was worse, he didn't say anything; just gazed at her.

In the end she spoke first. 'I'm sorry, dad.'

'You look awful. Are you hurt?'

'Oh no.' She looked down and saw her legs streaked with dirt. 'I've bin walkin' in the rain.'

'I didn't know what to do. I imagined all sorts of things.' It was her father who looked dreadful. 'I phoned Catrina around midnight. She said something was up - you had some sort of plan, but she didn't know what.'

'I wouldn't tell 'er. I was with a bloke.'

'I see. Not Barry, surely?'

'Course not.' She went across to fill the electric kettle and plug it in. 'D'you want a cup of tea?'

'A cup of tea? Oh God, what am I going to do with you, Tracey? Since you mother died I...' The strangest thing occurred. There was hardly any movement beyond the trembling of her father's shoulders, but tears started streaming down his face. She couldn't ever have imagined it happening. For a while he even pretended nothing was going on. Then he tore off a length of kitchen towel and rubbed at his cheeks like a man drying crockery. Tracey moved to put her arms around him. This hadn't happened either, not in a long time.

They sat facing each other across the table with their cups of tea.

'I'm sorry I said I was goin' out wiv Kat,' Tracey said.

'That's hardly the worst of it.'

'I don't like tellin' lies.'

'This man you've been with. What he's done is illegal. We need to find him.'

'I told 'im I was 16.'

'That doesn't excuse it. I can't bear to think...'

'Leave it, dad. They cover their tracks, these blokes. 'E was orl right.'

Her father was shaking his head. 'Anything could happen. He might have been violent. Suppose he made you pregnant.'

Tracey made a big show of drinking tea. 'I don't fink he could do that,' she said quietly.

'Why not?'

'Nuffink.'

'What do you mean, Tracey?'

'I just...don't fink 'e could. I missed me period last month.'

'I see,' her father said after a long moment. 'And that would be Barry?'

'Yes dad, it would.'

A long moment passed before either of them spoke again. She'd not been looking forward to breaking this news, and knew that he - like most fathers - would have hated to receive it. Yet she felt closer to him than for a long time.

'If you decided,' he said slowly, after a long pause, ' - I say "if" - that you wanted to end your pregnancy, I could cover the cost for you.'

'Thanks dad, but I couldn't do that. I couldn't kill it. I'd 'ave to 'ave it.'

'You're so young.'

'I've 'ad me fling tonight, 'aven't I?'

He nodded. 'You're a strange girl. Do you want to have it?'

'In a way,' she said faintly.

'And what about Barry? How could he help, do you think?'

'Oh gawd, dad, leave it out. You've seen 'im. 'E can't 'ardly look after 'isself. 'E'll be no use. Maybe a few years from now, 'oo knows.' She took a deep breath. 'No, I'll be on me own.'

He shook his head. 'Oh no you won't, Tracey.'

She was quiet for a moment, then reached across the kitchen table and held his hand. She sat like that for quite a time while the remains of her tea grew cold. She felt suddenly older than 15. Odd things were going through her head: Wordsworth's mad sister; Kat's mother cooking yams; herself standing half-dressed by the hotel fire door and her feet cold on the tiled floor; the waitress in the restaurant saying 'I'm sorry to hear that sir'. She fancied she could feel the baby growing inside her. It would soon be time for school.

~ Gary and the pole-dancer ~

The location for their after-work party was chosen by Wayne, and since he was the one getting spliced the others could hardly object. Anyway, as Wayne pointed out, what could be more suitable for a bunch of firemen than a club that featured a pole?

The younger blokes seemed comfortable with the notion of pole dancers, but Gary had never seen one and nor had his friend George. They sat on the fringes of the group watching a startlingly blond girl (surely she didn't eat enough?) whirling herself about. There was a lot of shouting and ostentatious drinking, and one of their mates came out with stuff unlike anything he'd ever said at work.

'What did Trish say about you coming to this?' George asked.

'Um...I didn't actually describe the place,' Gary replied. 'Thought it best not.'

'Aha!'

'Then what about you with Pat?'

'Well...the same, really.'

'See what I mean?'

'Didn't you tell me Trish saw some sort of Chippingdale act once? At a hen party?'

'She did, yeah. Well remembered, George.'

'So. She couldn't object to your coming here, could she?'

'That'd be logical, wouldn't it. You reckon women think like that, then?'

'I s'pose not.'

'Too right not.'

The etiolated blond waif had given way to a different girl on the pole. The new one was dark, stocky, and more energetic. Gary, who'd scarcely given the blond a glance, found himself paying close attention.

'Oh, so you like this one,' said George.

'She seems more professional. Foreign, I reckon.'

'She likes you,' said one of their mates, the station's champion basketball player. 'Can't take her eyes off you.'

'Oh yeah!'

But the observation was true enough. Gary had already become uncomfortably aware of it. However deftly the girl's body twisted and turned, her head swivelled so that the dark eyes were fixed upon him; almost as if the dance was staged for his personal benefit. It was so obvious that the other firemen started teasing him mercilessly. Gary was grateful for the subdued lighting because - for the first time in years - he felt a blush burn the back of his neck and spread to his face. It was curious because there was something about the girl that really did appeal to him. She wasn't wearing much, naturally - less as the act progressed - but the attraction was more about her face and the way she expressed herself; and, if he was honest, her looking directly at him like that, the dark eyes boring through him. When she whipped away the last garment and the men's eyes plunged irresistibly downwards, Gary's stayed hypnotically on her face.

'Another pint, Gary?' said George when the girl had taken a bow and vanished into a back room. 'Cold shower?'

'I'm OK,' Gary replied. Actually he felt disappointed by the dark girl's absence. The evening seemed empty after its brief offer of promise. When a third woman went to the pole he didn't bother to look up.

'Never mind, eh,' said George, who knew him too well.

Then Gary glanced at the corner of the room and the dark girl was there, dressed in jeans and a black top and putting coins into a one-armed bandit. He thought she looked even better in mufti. She looked wonderful. Surprising himself, he rose from the table and walked across.

'I hope you don't mind me saying,' he found himself commenting to her, 'But I really liked your dance.'

She hardly looked up from the machine. 'Thank you.'

'Look here.' He was thinking - God, it must be nearly 20 years since I've done this. An image of Trish crossed his mind but he let it go; no harm in talking to a girl. 'Tell me to go away if this is annoying you, but can I buy you a drink? My name's Gary.'

There was a clatter of coins as she made a small winning. She left the money there and regarded him with the calmness of a girl used to being chatted up. 'I am not annoyed, Gary. I am Andrea. Please, I like a vodka and tonic.'

Minutes later he was sitting talking to her, apart from the other firemen though with their comments ringing in his ears. It was ridiculous, of course. He could hardly believe it himself. But he'd asked, and she'd said OK.

'It's silly, I know,' he told her, 'But I felt when you danced that you were looking straight at me.'

She laughed. 'It is a thing the girls do. To make the concentration we choose one person, looking in him only. You have nice face so I choose you.'

'I see.' He was pleased and not so pleased by the explanation. 'You're not from England, are you? Can I ask where you're from?'

'Of course, Gary. From Brazil. A town called Goias. It is in the interior.'

'I've never met a Brazilian before,' said Gary. 'What does it mean exactly, when you say "the interior"?'

'It mean on the inside, away from the sea.'

'Like here in Edmonton. We're not on the sea.'

'That is different. In Brazil the interior can be very long way from the sea. Goias, it is one thousand kilometres.'

He looked at her, thinking he'd misunderstood.

'Yes, a thousand,' she repeated. 'This is why we Brazilians very sad people. We love the sea but living far, far away.'

'I can't imagine it,' Gary said. 'A thousand kilometres.' He couldn't help staring at her face, which wasn't at all the face of a pole dancer, whatever that might be. He'd seen all her body, down to a glimpse of - yes, even that - the little cleft between her legs, but her face was the sweetest thing; the least tarty face you could ever see on a woman. She seemed not to mind him staring. She was used to it, he supposed.

'Why did you come to Edmonton, Andrea?' he asked her. 'So far away. It's not beautiful here, is it?' He was thinking of traffic jams on the North Circular Road; the lorries piled up in a haze of petrol fumes.

'It is more beautiful than Goias.'

'Oh, really! Crikey!'

'Money, of course. I came for money.'

'I see.'

'Do you?'

'Not really.'

'Brazil is very poor country, and Goias very poor part of Brazil.

Nobody have jobs. My mother, she is sick, have no money for doctor. I have friend here, tell me "come to Edmonton, you get work", so I come. Now I am dancer.'

'I see.'

He kept saying 'I see' without seeing much at all. The new world opening up in his head was dimly illuminated. He envisaged a vast country covered in forests, with clearings for squalid little towns. The inhabitants were hazy, aside from the lovely Andrea.

'I suppose you've seen the sea in England?' he said.

'When the plane flew here one year past I saw it from the window. I have not been there. I am working here only.'

'But that's amazing, Andrea.'

'That is how it is.'

He bought her another vodka (more workmate jeers) and they went on talking. Any moment he expected her to move away, but she seemed content in his company. It was extraordinary how well they got on together. Gary liked fishing - he often went with George along the river Lea - and discovered that Andrea fished with her brother on a small Goiania river. Then they uncovered a mutual admiration for the recordings of Dr Hook. He started singing 'Years from now' and Andrea joined in; she knew more Dr Hook lyrics than he did. For some reason he started telling her about his uncle Reg's tall stories, and the same joke Uncle Reg told every Christmas (the one about a man who kept pancakes in a cupboard), and whad'you know but she had that sort of uncle too - uncle Joao - and he repeated jokes, and she told the one about two brothers who claimed to have caught the same fish.

Then came the moment Andrea laid a hand on Gary's arm and told him she had to work again.

'Work?' Gary was puzzled.

'My act,' she explained. 'On the pole. I must again do it.'

'Oh!'

This was an unexpected shock. Surely this sweet-faced girl who'd been talking about Doctor Hook and uncle Reg...surely she wasn't going to strip off the jeans and black top and reveal her naked body to all those jeering idiots. The notion filled him with repugnance and he knew he couldn't stick around to see it. At the same time a thought had been forming in his head; a ridiculous and most daring idea, completely untypical of him. And now - if ever - was the moment to mention it.

'Andrea, I have to go.'

'Oh - I am sorry.'

'But I have a suggestion. If you would like to see the sea, I could take you there one Saturday.' Saturday was good because Trish worked on Saturdays, and he didn't. 'There is a place called Hastings on the south coast. I could pick you up in the car and drive us there. We could see the sea and have some lunch and then come back. If you'd like to. It's just an idea. What do you think?'

She was on her feet ready to leave for the next dance, and Gary knew she'd turn him down. What a dope he was even to suggest it.

'You will take me to the sea, Gary?'

'Well yes, if you would like.'

'Next Saturday?'

'Next Saturday? Yes. Yes.'

'Thank you. I will like. I will like very much to see it. You have a mobile phone? Look, I will give you my number and my address, then you know where to come. It will be a nice day. I must go now, but I see you on Saturday, Gary. Ciao, ciao.'

*** *** ***

He arrived home soon after midnight to find the house in darkness. Trish, never a late bird, had gone to bed. He switched on the kitchen light and meandered through the lounge in the glare reflected through the connecting glass window, as he'd done many times before. Something about the shadowy room irritated him: the expensive 3-piece suite, the arid surfaces bereft of clutter, even the cleanliness. Neither of them were into reading, but it would have been nice to see a few books lying around. Something, anyway. It'd been better when Dominic was small, and a toy or two had escaped Trish's human vacuum routine.

He turned off the light, went straight up to the double bedroom, and undressed. Trish was asleep on her side of the bed. One shoulder remained exposed above the blankets, illuminated by moonlight from the window. She stirred as he clambered in but didn't wake. His body sank gratefully into the warm bed. Normally he dropped off as his head hit the pillow, but tonight this didn't happen. He knew why. Images of Andrea kept flashing through his head: her sweet face, and - admit it - her brown body, whirling round the pole. He tried to expunge them but the pictures kept coming. He felt randy as hell. There was nothing else for it. Gary eased himself across the bed and pressed his lips to the back of Trish's neck. Her head turned and a blast of smoker's breath scorched across the pillow; the habit he'd never persuaded her to relinquish. She groaned, still dead to the world, but Gary's patience was running out. He reached under the blankets and groped a buttock.

'Gary!' came her cry, awake now.

'Come on, Trish. It's been weeks.'

'What time is it?'

'What's that got to do with it?'

'I have to work tomorrow.'

'Come on. It won't take a minute.'

'Typical bloke. Bang, bang, all over. Go to sleep, Gary. Come barging in here pissed, crawling all over me. Leave me alone.'

He rolled away, breathing heavily, and had another try at sleep, which was a long time coming. He thought about 'taking himself in hand', as one of his uncles used to put it, but there'd been a time when Trish had caught him at that in the marital bed and kicked up a hell of a fuss. When he did manage to calm down it was the image of Andrea's face, not his wife's, that eased him into sleep.

*** *** ***

As Gary arrived home from his Hastings jaunt with Andrea, he saw Trish's car on the drive. He'd planned to get in before her but became stuck in traffic circumventing London. He parked and went in, finding Trish in the kitchen sporting yellow plastic gloves.

'Where've you been?' she greeted him.

'For a drive.' He had his story ready.

'What, on your own?'

'Just driving.' Avoiding an outright lie was important, he felt. 'There's no law against it.'

She gave the sort of look that wives give, then appeared to lose interest. 'I'm heating up some sausage rolls,' she said.

He left her to it, and went upstairs to sit on the john. It was the only place he could get away to think. A change in routine - he'd wondered about lying on the bed - might have aroused suspicion. He locked the toilet and sat on the floor with his back to the door.

He'd wanted to think about Trish and home life, but all he could see were images of Andrea: Andrea wearing jeans and a white shirt in the passenger seat of the car; Andrea laughing when he cracked a stupid joke; Andrea charging along the edge of the surf in bare feet; Andrea in the restaurant, leaning forward to shove a chip in his mouth. Andrea's face, over and over again.

Trish would go bananas if she found out; he knew that. Yet the day had been as innocent as a fishing trip with George. He and Andrea were friends; friends who got on well, shared a surprising number of interests, chattered and laughed together as naturally as... She was 17 years younger. Technically, he could be her father. Her father. It would be absurd to pin the label 'affair' on such a blameless relationship.

There was that kiss, of course. They were standing on the esplanade watching breakers crash onto the shore and Andrea had turned to him with spray in her hair and tears in her eyes and cried 'Thank you, Gary', and leaned up to kiss him on the mouth. He could feel her lips now pressing against his, the unfamiliar fullness of that sensation. How long had it been since he'd kissed anyone but Trish? He couldn't even remember.

How many years had they been married? Dominic was 19, so it must be 20. There'd been hell to pay when he forgot the score at their last anniversary. He'd never looked at anyone else. Some of the blokes at work chased after women, but it had never occurred to him. Even when

Trish started shoving him away in bed, he'd not been tempted elsewhere. He still found her attractive; still liked her, most of the time. Life was duller without Dominic at home, but that was something all parents had to get used to, wasn't it? He had the job, his mates at work, his fishing. He liked a bit of do-it-yourself at weekends, out in the back garden shed. There were spells of boredom, but the time passed. His expectations of life weren't so high.

Still - no use denying it - this little jaunt with Andrea had unsettled him. It wasn't just that he was walking around with a perpetual hard-on. That was plain silly: a middle-aged man remembering the lithe body of a young girl he'd got too close to. No, it was the fact of spending time with someone who could act so spontaneously; who could lean forward and kiss a man without thinking of the consequences; who had a whole life ahead of her and a hundred options along the way. And the contrast with his own existence, so set on its course, so unlikely to change. It had never bothered him before. Now the worm of dissatisfaction started to wriggle and it wouldn't stop.

*** *** ***

On Sunday mornings they breakfasted in the kitchen. Trish came stamping in - there was no other word for it - holding Gary's mobile phone in front of her.

'Who's this, Gary. This Andrea you've got a number for. Who is she?'

His heart thumped. 'What are you doing with my mobile, Trish?' he said, knowing it was useless.

'Who is she?'

'If you must know, it's a woman I met on Wayne's stag night. She's Brazilian.'

'Why've you got her number?'

'She wanted to see the sea. Brazilians miss the sea. I took her there on Saturday. I had nothing else to do.'

His wife's next words were lost in the piercing screech that came from her lips as she sprang forward and struck him in the face. Through the shock and the numbness of his cheek the one thought in Gary's head was 'Don't let on that Andrea is a pole dancer'.

'She was in our car?' Trish was shouting, out of control. 'In our car. I don't believe it. I'll never get in that car again.'

'You've got it all wrong, Trish. Nothing happened. It was a day at the seaside.'

The previous year, Trish had got involved with her boss at work. They'd slept together for a while, and then the affair got serious. One day she came home and told Gary she was leaving. She was gone several months and returned as suddenly as she'd left. Gary was so relieved to see his wife again that he took her back with minimal explanations. Another man might have brought up that time now and used it in his defence, but Gary was hopelessly naive. You could say he was under the thumb.

'I want to know exactly what happened on Saturday,' Trish raged. She looked like somebody else; like a woman Gary hardly recognised.

'I told you. Nothing happened.'

'You spent all day with her, didn't you. I want every detail.'

He told her, only omitting - he had that much sense - the kiss. If anything it seemed to make matters worse.

'I don't think I can get my head round this, Gary.' She was prowling up and down the kitchen like a caged tiger. Her face had turned a strange colour. 'I don't think I like this at all.'

'What can I do? Nothing happened, I keep telling you. But in any case, it was just a day out.'

'Don't use that tone with me, Gary. I'm not taking this lying down, if that's what you think. God, I simply don't believe this.' She plumped herself down at the kitchen table, then sprang up again. 'There's only one thing I can suggest. It may do some good or it may not. I don't know. You're to write down everything this slut said on Saturday...'

'She's not a slut...'

'Shut it, Gary.'

'She's not...'

'Shut up!' His wife sprang forward and struck him again, hard on the face. To his amazement, Gary found himself being turned on by it. For a second he considered throwing himself on her and tearing her clothes off. The moment passed and he reverted to the cowed husband. 'Just do it, and shut the fuck up,' she went on. Now his head really began to spin because Trish never swore. 'You're to write down everything she said...everything. I'll read it, and I'll see if it helps. That's all I can suggest, Gary, because I tell you, otherwise this could be the end for you and me. Now I'm going to bed.'

Another man might have asked his wife to write down everything her lover had said during her own affair, and that would have defused the situation. Instead Gary did what Trish asked him to do. At least, he tried to. A great deal is said in the course of one day, and simply remembering it all is a considerable feat. Being Gary, he tried to do it properly, without cutting corners. He went down to the newsagents and bought an exercise book and laboriously wrote Andrea's comments out in longhand. Since they represented one half of a conversation the text read strangely in places, but for the most part it held together. As the narrative grew he re-lived the day, and the more it continued the more he felt that Andrea's innocent role in the proceedings was being betrayed. When the last scrawled page was done and he put the pen down and sat back in the kitchen chair staring at the wall, Gary felt an unfamiliar feeling creeping over him. It took him a while to realise that he may have fallen out of love with his wife.

***   ***   ***

Gary baited the hook and cast his line into the murky depths of the river Lea. George, on his stool a yard away, sat staring pensively into the depths. No-one else was fishing, though a man could be seen exercising a whippet on the flat scrub 50 yards away. On the far side of the river a derelict warehouse sat in a thick patch of nettles.

'Could rain,' said George.

'Hope not,' said Gary.

He looked at the sky glowering over the black stretch of water and wondered what Andrea would have made of it. There were fish in the Lea, but that wasn't why they came. Maybe only someone brought up in Edmonton could see that this was the most appealing landscape within miles. He felt at peace here. It was more necessary than ever now.

'How d'you like your new flat?' George asked.

'I miss the shed.'

'D'you miss Trish?'

'It's hard to answer that.'

'You don't mind me asking?'

'I don't mind. She was becoming impossible, George. I had to get out. I get lonely sometimes...'

'Pat says will you come to lunch on Sunday?'

'That's very nice of her. She's a jolly good cook. Tell her thank you.'

'I will.'

'Now Dominic says he's goin' to move in with me.'

'Blimey. How d'you feel about that? You'll be out clubbing next thing.'

'I dunno. Believe it when it happens. It'd be strange at first.'

'I bet.'

Gary gazed along the concrete edge of the canal bank where, as a teenager, he used to ride his bike for a dare. He'd gone in once and arrived home in wet clothes. He didn't recognise the person who'd done that.

'Do you think you'll ever see the Brazilian again?' George said.

'Don't expect so. I did phone, but she's got this boy friend. She's 20 years younger than me. Silly, really.'

'You must be sorry you ever set eyes on her.'

'It's funny, you know. I really enjoyed that day in Hastings.'

They sat in silence staring at the black, still water of the Lea. If fish were down there they weren't remotely interested in the hooks and baits of the two men perched on the bank. The bloke with the whippet had gone home, and no-one else disturbed the yellow scrub. The sky released a squall of rain that briefly spattered on the surface of the river.

'I suppose Trish and I might get back together one day,' Gary said, almost to himself. 'I s'pose I imagined we'd go on as we were for ever. I never really thought about it. Something like this happens and...it kills the dream, doesn't it. Of course Andrea meant nothing to me, but she was a nice girl. The way Trish went on, I couldn't feel the same about her afterwards. If it comes to that, I don't feel the same about anything very much.'

~ Aswan bound ~

At mid-day the deck of the Anapurna was sunny and windswept, much as the young couple had anticipated from a Mediterranean cruise in December. They toured the bits of the boat that passengers were allowed on, then leant against the rail to gaze at the ocean. They could feel the thudding of engines on the boards under their feet. Gulls swooped onto the white caps of the waves. The young man had been worried about sea sickness, but the boat's motion was steady and that morning's large breakfast felt secure in his stomach.

A handful of fellow-passengers were on deck with them. The couple happened to be at the railing near the tall figure of a woman, similarly engaged in looking out to sea. The young man turned his head and saw that she was well past retirement age. She had a walking stick hooked over the metal rail.

'So exhilarating, isn't it?' the woman said unexpectedly. 'Such openness and freedom.'

'It's the way everything keeps changing,' he replied. 'I could watch it for hours.'

'Just as well,' said the girl. 'There's nothing else to watch.'

The woman laughed. 'I feel so liberated, after the life I've been leading. 'Are you two on your way somewhere - or is this a pleasure cruise?'

'God, not a cruise,' said the young man. 'We couldn't afford anything like that. I've been posted to a job in Beirut. My new employers are paying the bill.'

The woman leaned forward to address the girl. 'And what do you feel about this adventure?'

'Don't know really.' She looked absurdly young to the older woman. 'I had to look for Beirut in the atlas, to find out where it was.'

'What about you?' asked the young man. 'Where are you off to?'

'Egypt.'

'Right,' he said. 'Just visiting, I suppose?'

'No, I'm going to live there.'

'I see.' He tried to recall the Anapurna's schedule. Stops in Pompeii, Cyprus, Alexandria, Beirut. The woman would be disembarking at Alex. 'You know people there?'

'Not a soul.'

'I see,' he said again, not seeing at all.

He would admit, if pressed, to some nervousness about this Middle Eastern exploit, but he and his wife were supported by the organisation; tickets bought for them, couriers to meet and greet. Who would this elderly woman have to help her?

'I've never been abroad before,' she said, as though to echo his thoughts, 'Except for a weekend in Calais. 'I've led a very sheltered life as a house-keeper to my brother in Hendon. He was a parson. When he died...' She broke off. 'Do you really want to hear all this?'

'I'm absolutely fascinated,' said the young man truthfully.

'I'd have had to move anyway, of course. The vicarage always goes to the next incumbent. I had this dopey dream about settling down in Aswan. I thought...nothing to stop me now. It's 1960, not the 19th century. Get a grip, Frances. Do something, for once in your life.'

They stood there for a moment longer, watching the movement of the sea. Waves squelched against the side of the Anapurna sending spray into the air. One particularly heavy swell made the woman stagger, and the young man caught her arm.

'Thank you,' she said. 'I'm a bit unsteady on one side. It's this gammy leg.'

'Doesn't that make travelling difficult?' he said doubtfully.

'Sometimes. I had to miss out on Pompeii. I'd never have managed all those ruins.'

'What a pity,' said the girl.

'I can't have everything,' she said. 'At least I'm not sitting in rented accommodation in North London. I'm out here on deck with you.'

The next day the Anapurna arrived at Alexandria. They smelt the city before they saw it; an unfamiliar odour resembling rotting meat. Once the ship had docked, the uproar created by porters rushing on board swamped everything else. The young couple, waiting to go briefly on shore, saw one of them escorting the old lady and her luggage off the ship. She was negotiating the gang-plank gingerly, gripping the side with one hand and using her walking stick with the other. She didn't see them. Afterwards, they both wished they'd gone across to say goodbye.

The old lady had never been in a customs shed before, and was surprised to find this one masquerading as a small hut open at the sides. The porter laid her four cases horizontally on some wooden slats before a moustachioed customs official. A crowd pressed round. A thought about pickpockets crossed her mind, but then the official pointed at one of the cases and snapped out a word, which she realised was 'Open'. She fumbled for the right key on her key-ring, and turned it in the lock. The official's helper snapped it open and threw back the lid.

'Open,' said the official again. He was pointing to a small package that lay on top of a pile of clothes. He had the glowering expression of a man whom it was best not to cross. A policeman stood by holding a rifle. The whole scene was faintly menacing.

She watched while the helper opened the package, which simply meant unwrapping a paper bag. What on earth was in it? she wondered. The crowd wondered too; some of them craned forward to get a better view. Was it her imagination or did she notice a collective holding of breath until the moment the package's contents were revealed? As the helper shook them out she began to giggle. She'd been having some trouble with her rear end (as her mother always used to call it), and just before leaving had gone down Hendon High Street and bought two packets of suppositories. They lay there now on top of a familiar skirt which - she realised already - would be much too heavy to wear in the Egyptian climate. She tried to stop laughing but her shoulders were shaking furiously. She hoped the official would not interpret this as disrespect. Then she saw that the man next to her was grinning. Towards the back of the crowd someone else started to chortle. Did any of them know what the package contained? Unlikely. It was simply a matter of laughter being contagious. The sounds of sniggering took hold like a straw fire. Gusts of it swept the press of onlookers in the little customs shed. The policeman's rifle began to tremble. Now even the official's saturnine features split open, and a row of stained teeth appeared beneath the moustache. He barked an order, so that a minion snapped the cases shut and made four rapid chalk marks on their lids. She was in. Egypt had embraced her.

    Frances had thought carefully about what to do upon on arrival. She reckoned that on this first morning, while fresh and rested from the boat, she should get some travelling done straight off. A taxi was called, and while she leant on her stick amongst a seething melee of humanity, a porter in bright red clothes loaded the cases into the boot. She had no Egyptian money but gave the man a dollar, which seemed to go down well. At the railway station another porter got the cases out and put them onto a train for Cairo. Throughout these manipulations Frances watched the luggage possessively; the only visible link to a past that already struck her as remote.

The railway carriage was air-conditioned, up to a point, and tiredness was kept at bay by her fascination with an unfamiliar landscape: the flat greenness of the delta, with men in dish-dashas bent amongst the crops; then the desert, and its unremitting yellowness, so remote from anything seen on Hendon Ridgeway. But when she stepped from the train at Cairo station, the heat and strangeness of it burst through all her defences at once. Blindly, she followed her third porter of the day across the station concourse, struggling to match his pace (though he had the cases). Once, the porter stopped and said something, pointing to the uniformed police with dogs stationed at every exit. She understood so little of what was going on around her.

Into a taxi went the cases, herself following; then came a madcap dash through streets congested with all manner of traffic and livestock, until the driver drew up outside the Nile Hilton hotel, the name she'd given him. He had to repeat the amount of the fare three times, which - when she understood it - took her breath away. But she paid and, flanked by two more men with the cases, walked into by far the biggest hotel she'd patronised in her life. Recent terrorist outrages had meant some bargain prices for tourists, but the Hilton was still a daring step for the likes of her. No matter. Frances had promised herself two days of living it up, no questions asked, and she was damn well going to have them. She actually framed the word 'damn' in her mind. Was she a liberated woman, or what! Stanley would have had a fit.

In her hotel room she propped the pillows against the headboard of the bed and sat on the covers resting. Her leg felt tender, though little worse than it had after a morning's shopping in Hendon. She pulled on a cardigan to counter the effects of the air-conditioning. Beyond the unfamiliar, low hiss of cold air, a muffled honking of car horns from the road outside drifted through her closed windows. She picked up the TV remote control from the bedside table and press the power switch. On came a picture of men worshipping in a mosque, with a commentary in Arabic. She turned it off again.

She'd bought a couple of postcards down at reception, and began to write a message to Norah Trainer - because she'd said she would, rather than from any desire to communicate with the woman. Needing something to rest the card on, she opened the drawer of the bedside table and found a Gideon bible. Norah would have liked that. She had been a constant thorn in Stanley's side, the sort of devout, tiresome parishioner that every vicar had to tolerate. 'You can't imagine how different everything is...' she wrote, wondering whether to compare the air-conditioning with the draughts that both of them had experienced in the vicarage lounge. As her biro progressed across the postcard, Frances experienced a wonderful, guilty thought: this was the last communication she would ever have with Norah Trainer.

Close on the heels of this came another thought, a much bigger one. She would never again have to assume the mannerisms of faith that Norah carried off so dutifully: the iteration of certain ideas, the respectful tread in church, the modest inclination of the head. Stanley was dead. Frances was sorry about that - very sorry, actually - but it meant that he could no longer be embarrassed by the proximity of a sister who was a non-believer. And that was the truth of the matter. Let it be stated at last: she didn't believe. Put it more honestly, Frances, she told herself. She rejected, she actually rejected the whole paraphernalia of arcane belief and ritual that had underpinned her life for the past 40 years. She rejected it, and out here in Egypt nobody gave a damn. Frances shifted on the bed and gave a squeal of emotion, possibly delight.

Now she began to feel hungry. Six hours had passed since she'd eaten, and it was well past her normal time for dinner. A room service menu lay nearby with details in Arabic and English, but Frances had no wish to eat in the company of a blank TV screen and a Gideon bible. She felt suddenly lonely. For the first time in her life - the thought had just occurred to her - there wasn't a single person she knew within hundreds of miles. A meal with other unknown diners on other nearby tables seemed desirable. She changed into clean clothes and took the lift down one floor to the restaurant.

After she'd chosen and ordered, a man entered the restaurant and took the table next to her. It surprised her slightly as the room was only a quarter full, but of course people had a right to sit wherever they wanted. He was silent until her third spoonful of soup.

'Good evening, madame.'

Frances inclined her head to the man, who sat on her left. 'Good evening.'

'Madame is alone.'

'As you see.'

'It is unusual.'

He was about her age, a man with a lined forehead, a brown skin, and quite a luxuriant moustache. Something about him suggested that above the smart suit and tie should be one of those red fezzes that Egyptians wore in the old days. Should she be sitting here permitting a strange man to talk to her? Frances had no idea.

'If you would rather not talk, I understand.'

'I don't mind,' she said, after this clever defusing of a possible objection.

'I am Abdul.'

'I am Frances.'

He got to his feet with some ceremony, gave quite a deep bow - she imagined the fez falling off - and shook her hand. 'May I be bold and ask, Madame Frances...how is it you are sitting alone here in the Nile Hilton restaurant?' He came out with this sentence whilst regaining his seat.

What she said next astonished herself. 'Forgive me, Abdul, for I know nothing about Egyptian etiquette. But if we are to have a conversation without both getting a crick in the neck, it would be much easier to have you sitting opposite me. Is that permissible? What do you think?'

He rose for the second time, bowed again, and seated himself opposite without any fuss. 'What I think is...'

'The reason I am sitting here alone...' She told him about Stanley and the vicarage in Hendon; about the Anapurna and the trouble with customs; about her imminent visit to Aswan. She even told him about Norah Trainer. He nodded and smiled and said 'Yes', but didn't once interrupt. He was either a good listener or bored out of his mind.

'Madame is intrepid Englishwoman,' he said eventually.

'Oh, no! I'm just a desperate person.'

'I do not understand.'

'I'm not sure that I do.' She had not expressed all of these ideas before, even to herself. Especially to herself. When you depended economically on a certain life-style, certain things must be left unthought. They came out now under the truth drugs of solitude and palm trees. 'Where I went wrong,' she continued, 'Was after leaving school. Stanley asked me to be his house-keeper, and... I should have said "no". I didn't use my imagination. Years and years of that draughty vicarage, and tea parties, and the church flowers committee, and visiting the sick - oh, I didn't mind that, but - and all those services, two every Sunday.' An infuriating tear seeped from her right eye, and she dashed it away with the table napkin. I didn't believe all that stuff for heaven's sake. The virgin birth and the holy trinity and the bloody resurrection - oh, I'm so sorry...'

If she had ever in her life sworn before, no memory of it remained. But Abdul was unmoved.

'It is all right, Frances. Your religion is not my religion...'

'Not my religion now, but...'

'Anyway. I cannot be offended.'

'No. I've offended myself. Stanley would be so horrified. I'm sorry, dear.' She began looking up, then corrected herself. 'Oh goodness...'

'Take a moment. The ladies' room is over there.'

'Yes.'

She stumped across to the toilet - he elaborately pretended not to notice her bad leg - and dashed some water on her face. The long, thin features looked back at her in the mirror, wisps of damp hair pressed to her forehead. She looked like Virginia Woolf in the act of drowning, was the thought that occurred. She was glad Abdul had joined her, never mind which taboos had been broken. He had manners and was a good listener. All the same... Who was this man? The realisation came that she hadn't the slightest idea.

'I've been banging on about myself,' she said, rejoining him, 'And not asked a thing about you. Do forgive me.'

'Very boring person.' Abdul's order had arrived, but he'd waited for her before starting. 'Coming from rich family in Minho. You know Minho?'

'No.'

'South of Cairo place. Me? Buying selling, buying selling, all my life. Visit Cairo every month, always staying in Nile Hilton. Always in same room actually. Very boring man.'

'Are you married? Do you have children?'

'I was married for 25 years until my wife died. Children I have, grown-up. They have children. Many grandchildren, cousins, and cousins of cousins. Nieces, nephews, aunts and uncles. Standard Egyptian family scene. You cannot imagine.'

'No.' She grinned across the table. 'But I hope I'll find out about such things. In time.'

'Then you will wish you are back in the vicarage.'

She took a deep breath. 'I don't think that will happen, but we shall have to see.'

She finished her main course and he - a little way behind - finished his. She chose a dessert, more so that she could go on talking to him than because she wanted one. Then coffee. He showed no inclination to go, anyway. It seemed a very long time since she'd been so relaxed in someone else's company. We shan't be meeting again, she thought, so nothing matters.

Then he said two things which did matter.

'We are sitting at the same table,' came the first of them, 'So please...I wish to pay the bill'

'You mean pay for us both?' She was astonished. 'Of course not.'

'I said from a rich family I am come and it is true, you know. Filthy rich. Most of it I have not earned. The money is just there. I shall not notice one bill from restaurant, that is for sure.'

'It's not the point.'

'I am thinking maybe you will need the money later on.

'It's not your business to be thinking about my finances.'

'Of course. Of course. I am extremely sorry if madame is offended.' Despite the emollient words, he did not look at all sorry. 'Then I have another suggestion. Money is no part of it.'

'I hope this a more sensible one.'

'Who knows. It is hard to read madame's mind about such things.'

'Well?' (She was back to being 'madame' again, Frances noted.)

'I am staying at this hotel and so is madame. It would be possible for madame to visit my room after dinner and no-one would know.' He waited, and they stared at each other. 'What does madame think?'

Frances reached out one hand for her stick. She rose from the table impressively upright, like a rocket from a NASA launching pad. 'I have very much enjoyed our conversation,' she said from the standing position, 'But now I must retire for the night.'

He stood too, bowing gravely. 'I am sorry, madame.'

She settled her bill with the waiter and took the lift upstairs. In her room she lay on the bed with the lights off and the coverlet round her shoulders. The curtains were open and the waters of the Nile were visible beyond the maelstrom of traffic headlights. She was smiling. What had happened in the restaurant...well, it was the first time in her life that someone had proffered the suggestion of sex. It was absurd, of course - a dried-up old stick like her, and Abdul had behaved appallingly, but she was grateful to him. She'd even started to feel sorry for the man, wasting his evening on such a ridiculous wild goose chase.

The phone rang on her bedside table.

'Yes?.'

'Don't ring off,' said Abdul's voice.

'How did you know my room number?'

'The filthy rich can find out things. It is one of the advantages.'

'I see. Why have you phoned?'

'I want to give you the name of a hotel in Aswan. It is quite cheap but a nice hotel. It has a view of the river. You will need to look for a house, I expect, and this hotel, it can be a good temporary place.'

She was touched that he had taken this trouble; had thought about her situation and then offered some practical help. 'That's very kind...'

'Do you have a pen?'

She noted down the name and address.

'When will you go to Aswan?' he asked.

'Tomorrow.'

'If you wish, I can make sure they reserve you a room.'

'Can you do that?'

'I know the owner...one of my nephews.'

'Oh!'

Now she wondered if it was some kind of accommodation scam. She was so helpless, drifting lamely about this incomprehensible country. She thanked him anyway, and he wished her a courteous good night.

She woke the next morning feeling surprisingly refreshed. Hotel reception advised that there was a train to Aswan at 11.30. They also pointed out that the Egyptian Museum was just across the road from the hotel. Greatly daring, she decided to spend half an hour there before taking a taxi to the station. As she left the hotel's air-conditioning, Cairo's humidity closed upon her like a blanket. The unsuitable western clothes, purchased in Hendon High Street, sagged and clung to her limbs. Dust whirled about from the traffic. She was three yards across the zebra crossing before realising that it carried no authority in Egypt, and retreated as fast as leg and stick would allow. For a while, crossing those few yards in the face of oncoming cars appeared to be an impossible prospect. They were detouring at her deliberately, she thought, until she noticed the missing manhole cover in the middle of the road. A horse-drawn cart passed, its only load a pile of bones assailed by a furious mass of flies.

The high ceilings of the Egyptian Museum, once that building was eventually achieved, afforded coolness and a restful gloom. She joined the other tourists - there were no Egyptians - in ambling around the shambolic exhibits, hearing shoes clack on the stone floor. She started a foolhardy climb up the staircase before her leg gave out. Leaning against the rail prior to making a descent, she noticed that the heads of priceless statues were splashed with paint, legacy of careless local decorators.

By the time she hauled herself onto the train at Cairo station Frances was beginning to regret her jaunt to the museum. And an hour into the long journey her only thoughts were of its end. They had warned her about Egyptian stomach upsets, but the involuntary burp outside Minho (Abdul's home town) presaged a spiral of decline more rapid than she'd have thought possible. Lolling in the old-fashioned leather seats, she experienced the awful dissolution of her insides. The yellow - always yellow - scenes beyond the dust-stained windows swam in her fevered vision. Half a dozen times she tottered the short distance to the toilet, beyond caring about the stench and the grotesque condition of the floor. Once she passed out there, recovering consciousness in a posture that would have gratified a contortionist. She marvelled at the amount of liquid that could leave one body.

In Aswan she had to be roused from an uneasy doze to clamber from the train. It seemed like another elderly woman altogether whose luggage was loaded into a taxi, and who rummaged in her handbag to find the address that Abdul had read out over the phone. In the small hotel they recognised her condition and helped her up to the first floor room. She fell asleep fully dressed, cradling in her arms a bowl provided by the chambermaid.

When Frances woke the next morning she could not immediately identify her surroundings. She had taken in very little the night before, and felt so different after a night's sleep. She felt well! She felt hungry, for goodness sake. Her long legs swung from the bed and took her tentatively across to the shuttered windows. They were a typical middle eastern arrangement, the upper halves of two doors which opened onto a small balcony. She pushed them apart and gasped. The Nile was beneath, winding peacefully past with a few dhows scattered on the surface of the water. There was a hushed quality to the scene, the more noticeable after her memories of Cairo traffic. In that instant, standing barefoot in her crumpled dress, she thought: whatever happens now, I'm glad I came. She realised with a twinge of guilt that Hendon had not figured in her thoughts for the past 24 hours.

Someone tapped on the door, and she opened it to find a man standing outside, hands folded in front of his chest.

'Does madame wish to breakfast in her room or downstairs?'

'I'll be down in ten minutes if that's all right,' she said.

There were two other single women in the breakfast room, a sunny space looking onto the river. The hotel owner fussed over Frances, pressing her to accept more than the standard breakfast of coffee and rolls.

'You're popular,' said the middle-aged English lady at the next table.

'How did you manage to find this place? It's the best-kept secret in Egypt?'

'I was very fortunate.' Frances told her about Abdul.

'Oh yes,' said the lady. 'A nephew. Always the best way.'

The breakfast room had a small terrace attached to it, and after eating Frances went out there to stare at the river. An idea had occurred to her. She returned inside, spoke to the owner (who did a good deal of nodding), then went up to her room and opened one of the suitcases. Within 20 minutes she was seated on the downstairs terrace with a box of water-colours, a folding easel (unfolded), and a large sketch-pad. She felt wonderful sitting like that; peaceful, but at the same time stirred by an unaccustomed energy. All the same, after half an hour she screwed up her first attempt and started again.

An hour-and-a-half later the owner ventured onto the terrace. Approaching tentatively, he stopped two feet away to peer over her shoulder.

'Excuse me, madame. Very sorry to interrupt. I have make suggestion.'

'Oh!'

'This picture...'

'It's not very good.'

'It is very good, believe me, madame.

'I'm glad you think so, but I can do much better.'

'Yes madame. If I may say, there is a shop here, it is selling pictures to the tourists. My brother, he is the owner. Picture like this one...easily he can sell.'

'You really think so?'

'I am sure, madame.'

Frances looked at what she had done. 'It's nearly finished, and then it will need half an hour to dry. If you like, I can let you have it after that. By all means talk to your brother. I'd be interested in what he has to say.'

She took a short walk along the river front, then rested all afternoon. When she came down for afternoon tea the owner approached her, holding the painting in front of him. 'My brother, he like the picture. He offer you 50 dinars. Like I told you, madame. He say you do more pictures he like to buy them also.'

'Goodness!'

Frances had painted on and off all her life. She had a talent for it that had never been properly indulged. Hendon was not rich in scenes that excited the imagination, though a picture of her brother's church had hung in the vicarage lounge for 20 years. Selling paintings! That was an entirely new notion. Her financial arrangements for Egypt were precarious, to say the least. She'd had her modest savings transferred to a local bank in Aswan, and her small private pension would follow in the same way. Could she really supplement these slim resources by selling water-colours to tourists? It would make a considerable difference. What was more, she enjoyed painting.

'Goodness!' she said again, wondering whether she ought to bargain.

The owner reached into his pocket, withdrew a bundle of incredibly grubby notes, and counted five of them into her palm. The sight of the money swayed her judgement.

'All right then. Fifty dinars.'

Over the next few days Frances enjoyed herself as much as she could ever remember. She ought to be doing more, a voice of conscience told her on and off. She ought, at least, to be investigating accommodation. But it was so pleasant making little excursions by the river, as far as her leg would tolerate. So nice sitting on the hotel balcony painting, or just watching boats on the water. Who would have thought that such minuscule fluctuations of movement could prove so absorbing? And the hotel owner was so attentive, fussing round her in a way that nobody had done for years; well, no-one had ever done, if she was honest. She felt fitter than she had for a decade. Even the wretched leg ached less. When conscience reared its head, Frances told herself she was working, and working in a way that was more real than housekeeping for Stanley had ever been, because the outcome was money; small bundles of notes placed in her palm that put a value upon her existence. The work was improving too. The seductive, so-unfamiliar surroundings, the regular exercise of her craft, had induced all sorts of experimentation. She was growing.

After she'd been in Aswan for a week she returned to the hotel from a walk and was met at reception by the owner.

'You have a visitor, madame.'

He pointed into the breakfast room, where Abdul was comfortably seated at a table enjoying a pot of coffee and an Egyptian delicacy that involved a lot of nuts and raisins.

Frances was enormously pleased to see him. As she advanced to shake his hand, Abdul rose and - with a gesture she remembered well - bowed deeply. He spoke to the hotel owner, who hurried away to fetch more coffee.

She sat at Abdul's table and set about dispelling the awkwardness of their previous leave-taking. 'If you would prefer to take your refreshment in my room,' she told him, 'I would be honoured'.

He bowed again, comically, from a seated position. 'Thank you, madame. I am much appreciating your invitation and how it shows confidence in me. But I must tell you my nephew is the most terrible gossip. We will do well to stay in the breakfast room.'

She smiled. 'As you think fit, Abdul.'

'Now tell me how it is you are getting on here.'

She told him about the journey down, how happy she was in the hotel, how little she'd done to find accommodation, and how she had begun to paint. When the owner returned with the coffee Abdul talked to him again, this time in Arabic. The conversation lasted several minutes and Abdul began to speak quite sharply. The owner hung his head. He went away and returned with one of Frances's paintings. Abdul took the picture across to the window, balanced the frame on a table and stood studying it .

'So good,' he said to himself several times. 'So good.' There was more discussion with his nephew. At last some form of agreement seemed to be reached.

'I am sorry, madame,' said the owner, looking thoroughly miserable.

'Why are you sorry?' Frances asked.

'I will explain,' Abdul said. 'You may go now, Hashim.'

'What was that about?' said Frances, when they were alone together.

'In future he will pay you 70 dinars for a picture of that size. More if the picture is bigger.'

'Oh!'

'He is a good boy, but he is an Egyptian.'

'Oh!'

'When he takes your painting to his brother, he keeps a percentage of the profit. That is reasonable, but he is taking too much. Of course, you can take the pictures directly to his brother yourself if you wish...'

'But I don't want the trouble.'

'No. And in any case, he will adjust the price of the room here to take account of this picture business. But you must remember Frances that Egyptians, we are a friendly people, but money is always the most important thing. It is...I think you say, the bottom line.'

'Is that so, Abdul? Then perhaps you would explain why you have been so wonderfully kind and helpful to me when no financial gain to yourself is involved.'

'That is because I am a very bad Egyptian.'

'And what exactly does that mean? A bad Egyptian?'

'I am not sure. We should not look into it too closely.'

'Hmm.' She gave him an old-fashioned look. 'When you looked at my picture just now, you seemed to like it - unless of course you were just being polite.'

'I was not being polite.'

'And what does that mean?'

'I liked it very much.'

'Are you sure?'

'I assure you.'

'Then the next one I paint will be for you.'

'That is very much kind, but I could not possibly accept.'

'You will accept. You are not the only one who can do things for other people. When are you leaving Aswan?'

'I thought I would stay three nights. I have a house here.'

'Then the picture will be ready for when you go.' She raised a hand as he began to protest again. 'No, do not say another word.'

He sat quietly for a moment as if submitting to reproof like a child, then looked up. 'May I say a word on another subject?'

She smiled. 'Of course, Abdul.'

'Two other subjects, actually. First, there is someone I know here who has small flats for rent which I think might suit you...'

'A nephew?'

'A cousin, actually. I would like you to meet him. And secondly, if you could accept an invitation to tea at my house tomorrow, there is someone else I would like you to meet. An English lady. A friend of a friend.'

'Of course I accept.' Frances experienced an extraordinary sensation, as though - it seemed silly even to think it - her heart was literally filling up. 'You are so very, very kind to me, Abdul. I don't think I have ever...'

He executed one of his little bows, and rose from the table. 'Have you already forgotten what I warned you about with Egyptians, Frances? Do not ever suspect them of kindness. You will certainly be wrong. I will pick you up here at three o'clock, English time, if that is acceptable.'

The following afternoon he ushered her through the front door of his house not long after three. She had expected a dwelling that was large, given his self-proclaimed 'filthy rich' status, but no; it was modestly-sized, though - of course - on the river. The door was opened by a caparisoned servant; his head-gear was surmounted by a corrugated, triangular device like a large badminton shuttlecock. The lounge had a chandelier - de rigeur for all Egyptian households, as she was to learn - but was otherwise tastefully decorated. As Abdul and Frances entered, a lady who'd been sitting on the sofa got to her feet. Abdul introduced her as Rose. He offered the two of them mint tea or cardamom, then said he thought they would have a lot to talk about and that he would return in half an hour after clearing up some tiresome work he must do in his study.

'Well,' said Rose, as Abdul eased himself from the room. She must have been just into her sixties, Frances thought, and was slightly rotund in figure. Her face held a very open expression. Frances knew even from the declaration of the word 'Well' that she would like Rose, and hoped very much that the liking would be reciprocated.

'How did you come to know Abdul?' Rose asked.

'I hardly know him at all, but he's been enormously kind to me.' Frances explained about their chance meeting in the Nile Hilton. 'What about you?' she asked.

'It was more a second hand contact,' Rose replied. 'I never quite understood what, but there used to be a small commercial arrangement in Cairo between my husband and one of Abdul's family.'

'Another nephew?' said Frances.

'I think it was even a brother. When my husband died, Abdul found me a flat here - and this time it was a nephew. But it was Abdul who made the thing possible. You're right - he is a very kind man. Usually in Egypt it is hard to separate friendship from commercial profit. Not with him.'

The mint tea arrived - they'd opted for that - and they poured themselves a cup each. The windows were open onto the river, and a warm breeze fanned the napkins set out by the caparisoned servant.

'I wonder what Abdul meant,' Rose pondered, 'When he said we'd have a lot to talk about. You can be sure he had something specific in mind.'

'Heaven only knows. What did you do when you were in Cairo, Rose, if you don't mind me asking?'

'What did I do? Oh, you'd never believe it. That part of my life seems so long ago. I presided over tea parties, visited the sick, chaired the church flower committee...'

Frances began laughing, and it was quite a while before she stopped. 'I'm sorry,' she managed at last. Tell me, what exactly was your husband's job in Cairo?'

'He was vicar at the Anglican church there,' Rose said. 'For 20 years. For 20 long, bloody years, pardon my French. Don't misunderstand me. I loved my husband dearly, but all those tea parties...And you, Frances.

What about you? What did you do in England?'

~ Farewell ~

Foulkes, the most recent head of the Department of Information, nodded at the unruly ranks of men and women rising from the church pews and heading, not for the church exit, but towards the most likely partners for a gossip.

'Good turn-out,' he observed.

Foulkes's side-kick Stevens, soon to be undeservedly elevated to the rank of senior lecturer, curled his lip.

'The great and the good.'

Both men had loathed Arthur Davis with a passion, but a memorial service was not the place to say so. They were in a church, after all, and there was the question of propriety. An indelicate phrase overheard in the crush of bodies could easily have repercussions. In death, as in life, Davis had friends and enemies scattered about in roughly equal proportions.

As tended to happen at such ceremonies, the public man took precedence over the private. Still, the phrase 'the great and the good' was not entirely an accurate summation of the gathering. Certainly there were Vice-chancellors past and current, professors galore, leading figures from every corner of the UK information world. But also present were family members, including Davis's wife (often described as 'long-suffering'), and some mostly anonymous friends and sympathisers. For instance, who was this lone Jordanian girl snuffling into a handkerchief at the end of a pew, apparently unaware that memorial services were not designed for public displays of grief?

'Arthur was always full of surprises,' Professor Pillbright was telling two colleagues. 'I remember taking the London train with him a few years ago - for the IFLA conference, I believe. We were talking about the departmental research programme when Arthur turned to me and asked "Do you think I should marry Khelud?".'

The colleagues giggled in unison, then hushed as they remembered their whereabouts. 'What was your advice, Dr Pillbright?' one of them asked.

'I said it was a matter outside my competence.'

If that were the case, it would have been a rarity. Professor Pillbright was a polymath, a man so brimming with intellectual energy that he never watched television without reading a book at the same time. The passing years had slowed him physically but not mentally.

'And now Professor Davis can't marry anyone else,' said a colleague, hoping that Pillbright might reveal an opinion of his great rival. Pillbright was not to be drawn.

'We all have to go some time,' was all he would say. 'If you'll forgive me, I'd better have a word with the lady in question.'

Pillbright liked to bestow benefaction from a reasonable height, but for all that was a kindly man, genuinely concerned about the girl's welfare. He moved into the pew where Khelud still sat alone, lowering himself onto the wooden seat.

'I'm sorry, Khelud,' he began.

She blew her nose on a scrap of paper handkerchief and murmured something that was lost in the swirl of organ music.

'It must be difficult for you,' he tried again.

'I think of him still,' she snuffled.

'Of course you do.'

'He was good man, even though...'

'I know.' Pillbright did know some of it, and for the rest was content to remain in ignorance. Where Arthur Davis was concerned, he thought, a great deal might follow the words "even though".

'I am knowing him seven years,' Khelud said. 'He loved me still, I think.'

'Oh well.' Pillbright rose rather hastily, aware of Davis's wife standing ten yards away. 'I wonder, Khelud, now that you've finished your doctorate...will you return to Amman? You still have your job there, don't you?'

'Who knows?' she said dreamily. She could still feel Davis's hand on her breast, see his face a few inches away from hers; the all-seeing eyes, the little quiff of hair that gave him an eternally boyish air. When she went home, the dream of marrying an English professor would be gone for ever; whereas here in Leicester she could still imagine how it would have been, even with Davis's widow close at hand. She groped for another handkerchief.

Pillbright moved away and guiltily approached Monica Davis, who was standing by the font receiving a stream of condolences.

'How do you feel, Monica?' he asked.

'Unreal,' she replied. 'Arthur and I saw so little of each other in the last couple of years. I feel people should be commiserating with someone else.'

And so they are, Pillbright thought. Then he reflected that Monica would have known that, and his respect for her rose further. She was an immensely sensible woman who'd provided Davis with a solid foundation, something which - in spite of appearances - he'd badly needed. Altogether a much better choice for him than little Khelud. What Monica herself had got from the arrangement was harder to surmise.

'That poor girl,' she said, pointing her eyebrows in Khelud's direction. 'Can't she be persuaded to go home?'

'I've just had a try at that,' Pillbright said.

'Of course, he treated the little Jordanian girl disgracefully,' Foulkes was telling Stevens. 'The poor kid didn't know whether she was coming or going.'

'I expect she was coming some of the time,' Stevens observed.

The service was over, but few had left the church. Foulkes and Stevens had moved back from the nave, and were standing in a small alcove watching the movement of individuals from group to group, the pattern of gossiping; it would have made an interesting topic for a Masters dissertation, Foulkes reflected. Further back, the vicar was making unavailing shepherding motions towards the exit.

Stevens spoke again. 'I never understood how a man who wore sandals and socks in the summer months could pull so many women.'

'He did though, 'said Foulkes. 'There are several in the congregation today. And doubtless many more that we don't know about.'

Stevens, congenitally unsuccessful with women, shook his head. 'It's still a puzzle.'

'There was the professorial advantage - the attractions of power, and all that. And the direct approach was a help. Foulkes was known for his quick-fire analysis. Maybe some sort of sandal fetish in a couple of cases.'

The expansive figure of a black African moved into their orbit, obscuring the already dim light from the stained glass windows.

'Dr Mbanda!' Foulkes clasped the giant fingers, wondering whether Mbanda's resemblance to Idi Amin was just a figment of his imagination.

'A sad day,' Mbanda asserted loudly.

'Indeed,' said Foulkes.

'Professor Davis has made a major contribution to our department,' Mbanda went on self-importantly. The sentence might have been drawn from a published obituary. Foulkes wondered whether Mbanda had just written one for the *Nigerian library monthly*. Catch me passing my declining years in some fly-blown African library school, Foulkes thought. He'd once been out to Lagos - once was enough - and seen the clutch of sweltering classrooms that constituted Mbanda's department; had even seen Davis's broom-cupboard of an office. Oh no; when the time came, Foulkes would be out of the university in two shakes and straight onto the golf course.

Mbanda's thoughts were running on similar lines. 'Not every British professional would tolerate the discomforts of a Visiting Professor role,' he intoned.

'No, indeed,' Foulkes agreed. 'You know the expression "Dying in harness?"'

'What is "Harness?"' The accusing tone suggested that Mbanda should have been kept informed.

Foulkes explained about horses and carts. 'It's when someone works until the end.'

'Of course.' The African pulled on a pair of leather gloves preparatory to departure. 'But you have another expression - all work and no play makes Jeff a dull boy. I noticed a strange thing. For his - what do you say? - recreation reading, Professor Davis took only information science books from the university library. I have seen him one evening reading them on his veranda, glass of whisky by his side, not to worry about the mosquitoes.'

'That is dedication.' Foulkes did remember that Davis had once recommended the novel *Cold comfort farm*. Perhaps his reading of English literature had stopped there.

On the other side of the church Professor Pillbright was talking to someone called Carpenter, sent to represent the British Council. 'Such an engaging man, Arthur,' Carpenter said. 'I only wish he'd written more.'

'Or indeed anything at all,' Pillbright replied.

Carpenter, accustomed to the more tortuous style of British Council gossip, couldn't resist a small double-take.

'Don't misunderstand me,' Pillbright continued unabashed. 'Arthur was the man who started this department. Recruited the lecturers and kept order in the kindergarten. Filled the place with students from every continent. No small achievement.'

'No.

'We all write far too much,' Pillbright said. 'What sort of discipline is "library science" after all? Where's the science? Where's the content?'

'I suppose...

'Enough to warrant a City and Guilds diploma, but a Ph.D.? You haven't got one, I hope?' He touched Carpenter's arm to indicate that the question was rhetorical. 'Did you know Arthur well?'

'I liked him a lot,' Carpenter blurted out. 'I saw him on and off. We met when he came out to India. He was good to me. You know I was with him the day before he died?'

'Were you indeed?' Pillbright was interested in this. 'I knew he was in London.'

'Yes. He came into the Council and invited me for lunch. Took me to the Athenaeum, of all places.'

'Of course. He must have kept on his membership there. Dreadful food, I suppose?'

'The potted shrimps were OK. The thing is...' Carpenter felt himself being tugged into the current of academic gossip. 'Arthur looked a bit rough. He had several days of stubble on his chin, and was wearing a sort of windcheater affair. After we'd eaten, they gave *me* the bill.'

Pillbright laughed. It was a story he would enjoy re-telling. He took Carpenter's arm. 'It was nice for Arthur to have that last lunch with a friend. In fact it was a bit of luck that he'd come back from Nigeria on leave.'

With a small gesture - not exactly the sign of the cross, but a blessing of sorts - Pillbright indicated that the audience was at an end, and made his way towards the exit. He passed the vicar, whose expression said 'About time too' The few remaining stragglers were being flushed from the building. Foulkes, still attended by Stevens, stood by the doorway bidding them a proprietorial farewell. Pillbright would have passed by with a brisk nod, but Foulkes spoke.

'The end of a sad chapter, Professor. He could never bring himself to address Pillbright by his first name.

'Hardly a sad chapter,' Pillbright said. 'We all owe our existence here to Arthur.'

'In that sense, of course...'

'And when you think about it, most of us have struggled to emulate his considerable achievements.'

Pillbright walked on with the air of boyish enthusiasm that never left him. His insults were always indirect and unambiguous. He thought Foulkes a second-rater, unfit to utter a syllable of criticism against the department's progenitor. Pillbright had had his ups and downs with Davis, and everyone knew it, which was why colleagues had been tempting him to speak out all afternoon. But the movers and shakers in the little world of information had learnt to rub along together. He was sorry about Arthur Davis, and would miss him.

The vicar closed the door on the last, departing mourner and looked at his watch. There was just time for a cup of tea and a crumpet before his next duty. A christening, this time. He hoped it would move along more briskly than the memorial service.

~ Pod ~

The allotments sprawled below the railway embankment half a mile outside the village. Jack had rented a patch there for the past ten years. As far as growing things was concerned, he and his wife Patsy operated a clear division of duties: she was in charge of the back garden to their house, and he did the off-site stuff. On it he grew all the vegetables she didn't want to see 'littering' (her term) the garden proper. In spring and summer he set off there three or four times a week, sometimes every day. The place suited him. He felt a sense of useful cultivation on his patch of ground. He liked the gentle toil of allotment life; the measured pace of digging and planting; the slow exchange of views between the men, and the way they ganged up on mutual enemies like snails or greenfly. Above all there was the quietness; just the occasional clunk of a garden tool or the grunt of someone engaged in physical labour. Even the nearby railway line had its counter-attractions. When a goods train racketed past Jack would lean on his spade until the clack of iron wheels had faded into the distance.

'You sound cheerful.'

Stan had the allotment next to Jack's, and made a point of ribbing him about something or other whenever they met.

'Why wouldn't I?' Jack was unaware he'd been whistling. 'Look at these tomatoes, Stan. What d'you reckon?'

'Mmm. Dunno.' Stan sounded doubtful. 'Bit square-lookin' ain't they?'

'Square! Give over, you daft apath.'

'Any road, tomatoes is the least of your problems. It's that tree you ought to be worrying about. Thought you might've got rid of it by now.'

'Here we go.' Jack sighed. The tree was one of Stan's regular targets. 'Why would I do that? It's a lovely tree. Doubt whether you've seen the like.'

'Oh I 'aven't. And don't want to, neither. Look at it, Jack. Look at them pods, dangling there. Right peculiar. Gives me the creeps.'

The tree was certainly a novelty. It was all the fault of Carol, Jack's daughter. She'd done two years as a volunteer in Ghana, and at the end of it had turned up on her parents' doorstep with a plant in a pot (smuggled through customs, which Jack disapproved of). The idea was to bring something they couldn't possibly find in the UK. Carol must have been misinformed because it turned out not to be a plant, or even a shrub, but a small tree. Patsy banned the thing from the garden, so it went into the allotment. In the third and fourth years it grew quicker than a leilandia, shooting up to ten feet before abruptly stopping; a strange-looking affair with enormous, dark green leaves and the pods that Stan had drawn attention to growing in clusters around the trunk. If he were really honest Jack didn't much care for it himself. He thought that John Wyndham's fictional triffid might have looked very similar. Patsy, on a rare visit to the allotment, said she was afraid of it.

'You don't 'ave trees in allotments, Jack.' Stan was maundering on.

'It's not natural.'

'No law against it.'

'Oh no, you're within yer rights.'

'It's not keeping the sun off your cucumbers,' Jack said. 'That would be a crime, I don't think. Puts my rhubarb in the shade though, really does. An' you know what? The rhubarb loves it. Never had such a crop of the stuff, most of the year round an' all. We got rhubarb coming out of our ears. Patsy does it twice a week at least - rhubarb pie, rhubarb crumble, rhubarb and custard...'

'Rhubarb, rhubarb.'

'I can let you have some, Stan, if you like.'

'God, no.' Stan pulled a face. 'Can't stand the stuff. That's not natural either.'

'OK, suit yourself.'

***   ***   ***

Jack knew Patsy would be in the garden when he got home. It was a passion for gardening that had first drawn them together years before. Sure enough he found his wife on her knees by a flower bed. He approached quietly, watching her stab at the ground with a trowel.

Something about her intent manner and the fierce thrust of her arms took him back to those early days. He wanted to kneel behind and take her breasts in his hands. But the neighbour's wolf-hound was watching through the fence.

'Couldn't stay indoors on a day like this,' she said, hearing his footstep.

'Me neither. A grand day.'

'Make the most of it,' she told him. 'Another six weeks and the leaves'll be falling. Nights drawing in. Then a touch of frost in the air.'

'That's all right,' he said. 'I like that too.'

'Of course you do.'

'I mean it, Patsy. I like to see the cycle going round. Take the seasons as they come. I've always thought that.'

'All right, but if someone said - just supposing it was possible - if someone told you "You can have days like this one all the year round. The sun in the sky and a nice breeze but no cold winds and certainly no snow". I mean you'd take it, wouldn't you.'

He didn't need to think about it. 'No, I wouldn't,' he said. Then after a moment: 'Would you, then?'

Patsy took longer to reply, sensing that her answer would disturb the harmony of the moment; but she wasn't going to lie for him. 'Yes. Yes, dammit, I would.'

He cocked his head at her. 'So there's a surprise, after 36 years of marriage.'

'Thirty-seven.'

'You reckon you know what your wife's thinking...'

'You should be so lucky.'

'And all the time you haven't a clue.'

'But as no-one can control the seasons,' she said, reacting quickly to forestall him from sulking, 'There's no point in talking this nonsense, is there?'

He let it go. 'I'm going inside. Leave that wheelbarrow for me to handle. It gets heavy.'

'It's all right. I can do it. Tell the truth, I've not had so much energy in years.'

'Funny you should say that,' he told her. 'I'm the same. I was going like the clappers this afternoon. Put old Stan to shame. He asked what I was on.'

'And what are you on?'

'Let's see.' He poked about in the carrier bags brought from the allotment.' Tomatoes, spuds, the usual. What's this? Radishes. We can have those in the salad. Don't forget Carol's coming for dinner tonight.'

'I know that, you dope. What's in the other bag?'

'Can't you guess?'

Patsy laughed. 'Rhubarb, of course.'

'There's loads more out there.'

'Good. I can't get enough of it. I'll make a rhubarb tart.'

'That'd be nice.'

***   ***   ***

Carol arrived around seven. She was Jack and Patsy's only child and had grievously disappointed her mother by remaining single and - which was almost worse - childless. Looking at her personable, attractive offspring, Patsy couldn't think why this should be so. She'd long passed the stage of imagining that her daughter was a lesbian. And she'd lowered her sights about the acceptable qualities of a son-in-law, as long as someone came forward. She was even prepared to see Carol conceive 'out of wedlock', as they called it in her day. But of that there was no sign. In most other respects Carol had been a model daughter. She'd done well at school, gone to university, got a good degree then a good job (in town planning).   They told friends and neighbours she was a career girl.

When in company, Jack or Patsy would say that they 'didn't know where Carol had got her brains from'. (No-one from either side of the family had been to university before.) But privately Patsy thought the grey matter had come from her. Patsy was smart, and she knew it. She thought quickly and clearly. She saw things. There'd been no question of a proper education for her; it wasn't the sort of thing her family did. But she could - she felt sure - have hacked it at university. She could run rings round Jack when she wanted; she'd spent half her life trying not to.

That evening she made a pasta dish with a salad, including the radishes. When they'd finished it Carol jumped up to help with the plates.

'Leave those,' Patsy told her. 'There's a pudding. You'll never guess what.'

'Well...' Her daughter raised her eyebrows. 'Does it begin with R?'

'It might do.'

Carol laughed. 'You two. Dad's beginning to look like a stick of rhubarb...that green and red complexion.'

'Oi!' Jack protested.

'It's good for you, Carol,' said Patsy.

'It must be. Just look at you.'

'What do you mean?' said Patsy, knowing full well.

Carol leaned across the table. 'You look great, mum. You look really great.'

Patsy pretended to toss her head dismissively. 'Don't be soft, child.'

Jack spoke up too. 'You know you do, Patsy. No-one believes you're nearly sixty.'

'It's you as well, dad,' Carol told him. She got up and put her arms round his shoulders. She knew he liked that. 'You're positively blooming.'

'Girl's going daft,' he said. 'I'm over sixty, me duck. Time's marching on.'

'Well I know it is,' Carol said, 'That's why I wanted to tell you something.'

They recognised her tone; the special voice that meant she was going to tell them something. Patsy, coming in from the kitchen with the rhubarb tart, paused for too long and burnt her fingers through the oven cloth. She banged the dish down.

'I've met this bloke,' Carol went on. 'His name's Mark.'

Patsy was suddenly occupied with moving plates about.

'I like him,' Carol went on. 'He's 30 - a bit younger than me.'

'Five years younger,' said Jack.

'What does he do, love?' Patsy asked.

'He runs a think tank. A political think tank.'

'Blimey,' Jack said.

'They explore new ideas, mostly socialist stuff. Run seminars, publish papers, that sort of thing.'

'A bit intellectual,' Patsy said.

'You think I can't handle that?'

'Don't be silly,' Patsy said. I know you can.'

'I really do like him. I'm all up in the air about it, to be honest. It's been a while.'

'You don't have to tell us that,' said Patsy.

'Well I know. That's why I thought I'd warn you. I might bring him round some time.'

'Blimey,' said Jack again.

'Then I can tell him about grand-children,' Patsy said.

Carol grinned at her. 'Just you dare, mother.'

*** *** ***

A month or so later (Carol still hadn't brought her bloke round) something happened that made them both think. Two things, actually. They were lying in bed around midnight when Jack felt a powerful urge to cross from his side of the mattress onto Patsy's. He tried to resist the impulse. It was something he'd not done for quite a while. A chapter closed. Re-opening it now would bring complications. But the devil was back - that urgent, not-to-be-denied mood - and he was emboldened enough to roll across and place a hand on his wife's thigh.

'Hello, what's going on here?' came Patsy's muffled voice.

'Still awake, love?'

'I am now. What are you doing?'

'What d'you think, you daft apath? It's not been that long, surely?'

She turned to face him, now fully awake. 'Yes, it has actually.'

'I know, love. I'm sorry.'

'I've been wondering why we kept this double mattress. I've felt like the bedside lamp.'

'I know. I just got old, I suppose.'

'And now? Now that you're even older?'

'I don't know. It just came back. Don't ask me why.'

He moved to take her in his arms, but Patsy extended a restraining hand. 'Hold your horses, pardner. This'll take some adjustment. Are we talking a one-night stand here?'

'How about once every night?'

'Hmm. Look, I would like our love life back. I missed it awfully at first.'

'I'm sorry, love...'

'It's all right, Jack.' She patted his hand. 'But tonight...I can't.'

He half sat up immediately and she felt his concern; the concern that had always been there for her. 'Are you OK?' he said. 'You're not ill, are you?'

'It's not like that. I've been meaning to tell you since the first time. I thought it was some odd quirk to do with my body. Then yesterday it happened again.'

'What happened, Patsy?'

'Something that's been gone a dozen years at least - and good riddance to it - came back again.'

'You don't mean...?'

'Yes, I do. It's one of the few good things about getting old, dispensing with that monthly curse. Now...though I still don't believe this...it's back.'

'But you're 57!'

'Tell me about it.'

He drew his wife close and held her, now without the urgency of sexual intent. It felt good all the same. 'Maybe you'd better see Dr

Simpson tomorrow,' he told her. 'Just in case.'

'I was thinking the same. I'll give him a ring.'

'Good.'

He kissed her and went to roll back to his side of the bed, but this time his wife restrained him. She lowered a hand and manoeuvred it through his pyjama trousers.

'First let me deal with this,' she said. 'Lie still.'

***   ***   ***

Patsy phoned the local clinic next morning and made an appointment. Dr Simpson had the week off, so she was fixed up with a Dr Parker, the stand-in. She went along to wait her turn, then was called into the doctor's room. Parker was a smart-looking guy in a dark suit, more like a prosperous businessman than a doctor.

'Something odd has happened,' she told him without preamble. 'My periods have started again.'

'I see,' he said. 'So let me get this straight. They stopped for a while...then they re-started.'

'Yes.'

'It's not so unusual, you know. Assuming you're not pregnant...'

'No, no - of course not.'

'There can be several reasons why they stop. Did you lose weight, for instance? Maybe after some heavy exercise in the gym? Were you upset about something?'

'The thing is...'

'How long did they stop for?'

'Twelve years.'

'I'm sorry?' Dr Parker stopped the flow of questions and stared at her. He was like an actor who'd played the same part for years and had his lines changed.

'They stopped twelve years ago. I thought I'd finished with all that.'

'Forgive me, Mrs Bannister. Let me do what I should have done in the first place.' He turned to the computer screen, ran his eyes down her records, and frowned. 'May I check something with you? This date of birth we've got down here. If it were correct, you'd be...well, you'd be fifty seven years old!'

'That's right.'

'Fifty seven!'

'Yes.'

He started cleaning his glasses, as if they were to blame for duff information. 'I'm gob-smacked. If you don't mind my saying so, you look a much younger woman.'

'There's not many women would mind you saying that, doctor. But I'm 57 all right. I've got the lines to prove it.'

He put the glasses down and peered into her face. 'Age isn't about lines, is it? It's an attitude, an atmosphere. The way someone walks about, the things they say and how they say them. A mood...spring rather than autumn.'

'Steady on,' Patsy said.

'I know. I shouldn't. Tell me, have you been taking any potions lately? Any little phials of liquid labelled "Eternal youth"?'

She smiled at him.

He typed something on his keyboard, then turned back to her. 'I won't pretend to you. I've never met a case like yours. Most women start menopause between 45 and 55. Menstruation can stop and start again, for various reasons. But a 12-year gap...'

'What should I do, then?'

'I'll arrange for some X-rays, just in case. But not to worry. I can't believe there's anything seriously wrong with your body. Quite the reverse. The research people may be interested, mind you.'

'You mean I'm a freak.'

He turned to look at her again. 'Believe me, Mrs Bannister, if you're a freak all my other patients will want to go there.'

***   ***   ***

In due course Patsy had the X-rays. The doctors told her everything was normal. Her monthly cycles were back, sure enough, and she must get used to them all over again. And she had to think about birth control, bizarre as that seemed. These developments weren't as strange as they might have been because Patsy felt so good. They both did. Jack was in pretty good shape too. He even rejoined the over-40s kickabouts in the park, Sunday mornings, which he'd given up years before. He complained about feeling puffed, but he did it.

After the whole business was over they both reckoned they'd been slow on the uptake, but that was with the gift of hindsight. At the time they'd seen the gradual enhancement of their well-being as a sort of Indian summer, to be enjoyed while it lasted. The turning point came after they'd invited for lunch a couple of old friends whom they hadn't seen for five years. The apparently commonplace encounter started them thinking. The contrast between the relative appearance of the two couples - their friends' normal ageing against their own youthfulness - shocked them; and so did the reverse reactions mirrored on the faces of the other pair.

The inquest began the moment their friends departed.

'Right, my girl.' Jack took his wife's arm and drew her away from the front door, where they'd been waving at the departing car. 'Pot of tea, and we're going to talk this out. Kitchen table. Like we always used to.'

He brewed up and rejoined her with two mugs of tea. She noted the way he sat down, swinging his leg over the chair like a teenager.

'What is there to talk about?' she said.

Up he leapt again, and she heard him go into the downstairs toilet. He was back with the ornamental mirror they kept on the wall there. Without a word he held it up so that his wife could see the reflection of her own face. Patsy said nothing. She often looked at herself in the mirror - what woman didn't - but it was disconcerting when her husband stood by watching. She did look good; she knew that. It meant that others would think so too. Seeing herself at that moment, she felt a sense of her powers growing.

'All right,' she said. 'Take it away now.'

He put the mirror down. 'Dammit Patsy, we're actually getting younger. We look younger, we feel younger. Talk about it, why won't you? Why is this happening?'

'I don't know, do I? Some genetic quirk?'

'Both of us? If it was just you, maybe, or just me - but that's not it. We're from different blood-lines.'

'Then it's to do with where we live. The water supply, maybe.'

'No different from anyone else's. If it was water, other people would be affected.'

'I s'pose so.'

They sat in silence for a minute before Jack banged the table so hard that tea spilled from the mugs.

'Of course,' he said. 'Of course.'

'What?'

'Dammit, I should have twigged before.' Jack was positively chortling. 'It's been sitting there day after day before my eyes.'

She grabbed his arm. 'God, you're an infuriating man. What are you talking about?'

'It's not water,' he went on excitedly. 'It's food.'

'What do you mean?'

'The allotment, don't you see. What's in our allotment, Patsy, that nobody else has got?'

'It's the usual stuff - tomatoes, lettuce, spuds...'

'No no, the tree. The tree Carol brought back from Ghana. No-one else has got that.'

'No-one else would want it.' She thought for a moment. 'I still don't see. We don't use stuff from the tree, thank God. Catch me eating those pod things.'

'We don't, but the roots go down into the soil, don't they?'

She looked at him. 'You're telling me the tree affects other things you grow there. But if that's right, why hasn't half Africa been rejuvenated? Those pod thingies would be ten-a-penny over there. Why does it only work here?'

'Because, my sweet...' He leaned over the table. 'It only works together with one other thing. A vegetable. Is it a vegetable or a fruit - I've never known?'

She stared for a moment, then began to laugh. What started as a giggle swelled to a full-throated belly laugh. 'Rhubarb, rhubarb, rhubarb. Rhubarb,' she shouted. Before long Jack had joined her, and they sat guffawing like a couple of idiots. Patsy had tears running down her face.

'You must be quite clever after all,' she said eventually, 'To have worked that out.'

'It's high time you realised it,' Jack told her. 'So you get the picture? It's the pod tree and the rhubarb growing right underneath it. Rhubarb's a very English food, don't forget. You need a good frost to bring out the flavour. No-one would cultivate it in Africa. And we've eaten so much of the stuff. N'you know what's so funny about this, Patsy? The leaves of the rhubarb plant are poisonous. Isn't that an odd thing?'

Patsy didn't reply. Her thoughts were racing, tumbling over themselves in her eagerness to weigh up the implications of the discovery. She felt she stood on the brink of enormous developments, and wasn't a bit faint-hearted. Anything and everything that came from them would be all right with her.

Her husband was talking again, and she made an effort to pay attention. 'Imagine us going next door,' he was saying, 'Telling them we'd discovered a rhubarb recipe for eternal youth.'

'You'd have to say a bit more than that.'

'Oh don't worry, love. I won't. We'd find ourselves in the nearest loony bin. I shan't mention it to a soul.'

Patsy compressed her lips. So here it was, she told herself: the moment she'd known was coming. She looked at Jack, leaning comfortably on the kitchen table as she'd seen him a thousand times before. The word 'comfortable' suited him; amiable, at ease with himself. Then - it was no use, she must allow herself to think them - other words came: unimaginative, inward-looking...limited. Part of her wanted to spool the film backwards, to the point before she knew the ridiculous truth about rhubarb and pods. But she knew this couldn't happen. The wheels were in motion.

'Now just a minute, Jack. We can't leave this thing where it is.'

'You what?' he said. The expression had always irritated her.

'If you're right about this,' she explained patiently, 'We'll be telling people all right. We'll be telling a whole lot of people.'

'Now hold hard, Patsy...'

'You don't keep this sort of thing quiet. It'd be the biggest scientific breakthrough since penicillin. Much bigger than that.'

'It'd turn the world upside down, me duck.'

'Exactly.'

'Is that really what you want to do?'

'It's not a question of wanting or not wanting,' she said. 'It's there and we know about it.'

'And we're the only ones who do. If we don't tell, no-one else will find out.'

Her patience ran out, as she'd known it would. 'Oh for God's sake, Jack. This is the one chance in your life to make a splash...'

'Is that what you call it? A splash. Suppose I don't want to?'

'Well you wouldn't, would you.'

'An old stick-in-the-mud, is that what you mean?'

'You've not exactly set the house on fire.' They were still either side of the table, and she grabbed his arm again. She felt like seizing his neck. 'This business could be worth a fortune, don't you see?'

'So that's it.' He was angry now, a rare event. 'You've never got enough, have you?'

'Most people enjoy having money. Wouldn't you like a better place to live? A decent modern house?'

'I'm very happy here, thank you.'

'A Mercedes to drive?'

'There's nothing wrong with a Fiesta?'

'We could go on a world tour.'

'Skegness suits me fine.'

'Skegness.' Patsy bit out the word with utter contempt. 'Yes, there we have it.' She egged herself on into a fury. 'Well, you go right on...digging your allotment and reading your Daily mirror and supporting your stupid, silly little Leicester City with their other mediocre, pathetic fans. And while you're at it - while you're digging up your lettuces - I'll explore our discovery.' She thumped her breast. 'I'll explore the discovery that's going to change the face of the world.'

The kitchen sounded horribly quiet after she'd finished this speech. She'd gone too far, of course, and had done so deliberately. She'd needed a show-down. They'd been building up to one for some time; for 20 years or so. Jack sat there speechless.

'What are you going to do?' he said eventually.

'I'm not sure yet. Contact one of the big pharmaceutical firms, I expect. See what they think about it.'

'They'll laugh at you. They'll think it's absurd.'

'We'll see about that.'

'Do one thing, I beg you. Leave it for 24 hours. Think it over. Think through the consequences before you take such a step.'

She gave a twisted smile. 'All right then, 24 hours.'

'Thank you. And may God help us.'

***   ***   ***

The next morning Patsy woke with a headache. This was unusual, but she knew the reason immediately. Over the years it had been their policy not to go to bed on a quarrel, and for the most part they'd managed it. Yesterday had been a rare failure. The thought bugged her, but reinforced her determination to go ahead. When Jack had left for the allotment she searched Yellow pages and phoned a firm called Global Chemicals. There was the usual malarkey, keying in numbers and listening to recorded music. She asked for 'someone in the research department', but when a live voice came on the line it was Andy from Public Relations.

'No, that's not right,' Patsy said.

'I'm sorry?'

'Forgive me,' she said, 'But I asked for someone in research.'

'They tend to be very busy, Mrs Bannister. Can you talk to me first?'

'I'll try, but it's not so easy to describe. My husband and I have made a discovery. To cut a long story short, I want to sell it to Global Chemicals.'

There was a pause before the man said 'I see'.

'You must have loads of people phoning in like this,' she said.

'To be honest, it rarely happens this way. What's your discovery about?'

'You'll laugh if I tell you on the phone.'

'Try me,' Andy said. 'I won't laugh, I promise.'

'All right. We've discovered a way of making people younger.'

Andy's guffaw was surprisingly genuine for a PR man.

'You said you wouldn't,' she told him.

'I'm sorry. You took me by surprise. It sounds like a potion for eternal youth.'

'I wouldn't put it quite like that, but...well, it's along those lines.'

When Andy spoke again he sounded much brisker. 'Mrs Bannister, what are your credentials in this field?'

'Credentials?'

'I mean your qualifications for doing this kind of work. Do you have a background in the chemical or biological sciences? How long have you been engaged in research? That sort of thing.'

'Oh no, nothing like that. My husband's a retired postman. I'm a housewife.'

Andy laughed again. 'Why don't you write to me with a brief outline of your proposal. I'll pass it on to the right department.'

'No no. You'll just file it away. I want to talk to someone on the research side. Someone with clout.'

'Really, I don't...'

'If you can't arrange that, I'll go straight to another firm. And when the world hears about this discovery - which I promise you they will - I'll make sure everyone knows that Global Chemicals turned it down first. Do you think your bosses would be pleased about that? Would it help you to get promotion? Would you have a job left at all?'

There was another pause; a longer pause than was usual in the world of public relations. The PR man sighed. 'All right, Mrs Bannister, I'll talk to the research people and try and fix a short meeting. It may take a while...'

'This week, please.'

'If they agree, you'll have about 15 minutes to make your case. I'd advise you to have your evidence ready.'

'Thank you. You'll be in touch, then?'

'I'll phone you in the next 24 hours.'

In the event Andy was better than his word. He phoned back around tea-time, fixing an appointment for two days later. Jack was in the kitchen at the time, and overheard Patsy taking directions to Global Chemicals' London office.

'What was all that about?' he said when she came off the phone.

'You know what. I'm going to sell our secret.'

He looked aghast, then flared angrily. 'Oh no, you can't do that.'

'Too late. It's all fixed.'

He was furious. 'This isn't like you, Patsy. First of all, you agreed to wait 24 hours before making up your mind.'

'It'll be more than 24 hours by the time I go there.'

'That's not the point and you damn well know it.'

'To hell with it. To hell with you.'

'You lied to me. You've never done that before, not in 40 years.'

'Then it's about bloody time I did. And secondly?'

'What?'

'You said "first of all" in your pedantic way as though there was something else.'

'That's right,' he said. 'This isn't just your discovery. Actually, if push comes to shove, it's mine.'

'Come with me, then.'

'You know I won't.'

'What are you going to do, Jack? Bind and gag me?'

'I can't believe you're behaving like this.'

'I'm sure you can't, because you don't know me. You don't know what I want.'

'Would that be money, for instance?'

'Don't you want a share of the profits?'

'I wouldn't touch them with a barge pole.'

'That's perfect. I'll keep it all. The man who doesn't need anything has spoken. Now it's my turn.'

*** *** ***

Two days later Patsy travelled to London. The headquarters of Global Chemicals was a 20-storey building on the South Bank. She sat first in a circular atrium that had fountains in the middle, surmounted by a Henry Moore statue of reclining women. Andy appeared and led her into a reception room containing a table, chairs, and a young man introduced as 'Mr Saul, senior researcher'. To Patsy - despite her rejuvenation - young men still looked very young, and she guessed that Saul was actually a junior researcher. After a bout of introductions, Saul asked Patsy about her discovery.

'I wonder if you have any proof of your claim,' he said before long. 'That's always a paramount consideration.'

Patsy said: 'Tell me, Mr Saul, how old do you think I am?'

Saul gamely had a shot at it. 'I don't want to be ungallant, Mrs Bannister, but I'd say...mid-thirties?'

'So let's add at least five years for gentlemanly conduct,' said Patsy. 'That puts me in the early 40s. I'm actually 57.'

Saul stared. 'That is a surprise. Are we to understand that you've been "taking" your own rejuvenation method?'

'Without being aware of it, yes.'

'You don't look anywhere near 57, I grant you,' he went on, 'Perhaps you're one of those fortunate people who've always looked younger than their years. We're going to need rather more than that.'

Patsy opened her bag. 'Here's a copy of my birth certificate. Here's a photo of my husband and myself taken about ten years ago. The date's on the back. You'll see that I look rather older. Here's another taken a little earlier. Here's a photo of our daughter, Carol. She's 35.'

'Forgive me, Mrs Bannister,' Saul said, 'But I need to ask a rather personal question.'

'Go ahead.'

'Er...how much plastic surgery have you had in recent years? Face-lifts, nip-and-tuck, that sort of thing?'

'Oh, nothing like that. I used to have facials at a local beauty parlour but I stopped those two years ago. Oh, and I should have said - my periods resumed a few weeks ago, about ten years after they'd stopped. You can check that with my doctor. I've got his details here.'

'Just a moment.' Saul turned to the PR man. 'Andy, could you see if Patrick is free to come in for a moment. Fill him in on what we know already.'

'I'm on the case,' said the PR man.

'Dr Patrick Roche, head of research here,' Saul told her when Andy had left the room.

'So you're starting to take me seriously,' Patsy replied.

Patrick Roche, when he arrived shortly afterwards, was more the sort of figure Patsy wanted to talk to. He was about 50 and carried himself with unassuming authority. The others buzzed around him like nursing staff round a surgeon.

'I need to ask about method,' Roche said after the introductions. 'What exactly are you doing to effect these physical changes in yourself?'

Patsy hesitated. 'I don't want to give away the details...well, without...'

'Without a financial agreement,' he finished for her. 'No, of course not. But you must tell us more than you have. What sort of thing is it?'

'It's something we've been eating.'

'How long for?'

'About three years.'

'Eating regularly?'

'About twice a week, on average. For much of the year, anyway.'

'Mrs Bannister...assuming this is a standard food item...'

'It is and it isn't.'

'Why isn't everyone benefiting? Why aren't we all leaping about like lambs in springtime?'

'Because what we're eating...that thing has been affected by something else.'

'Some sort of pesticide or similar treatment?'

'Not really.'

'But something unusual?'

'Yes... quite unusual.'

'I see.' Roche paused, and Patsy felt that an important question was imminent. 'Tell me,' he went on, 'Where does this...accident happen?' She said nothing, and he prompted 'In your garden?'

It was on the tip of Patsy's tongue to mention the allotment, but she restrained herself. Lies had never come easily to her, yet she'd recently told one to Jack and now she trotted out another. 'Yes, the garden,' she said. 'Where else? Now look, I'm not willing to say more until I have an indication of price. After all, once you know what the discovery is you could go right ahead and develop a product without me.'

'That's not how Global Chemicals operates, Mrs Bannister. Any agreement we draw up will state, on the one hand, what you're going to deliver - essentially the concept, which we should need to test over a period of years. On the other hand it will state what we deliver to you - essentially your fee and the timing of the payment.'

'And what might the fee be? Patsy said.

'That will need to be negotiated.'

'I need some sort of idea. I was thinking why don't you say a figure, and I agree it, or not.'

'That's what negotiation is about.'

'So...?'

For the first time, Roche looked less than sure of himself. 'If your claim has any validity,' he began. 'Well...from what you say there have been no start-up costs. Few costs of any kind, apparently.'

'Could you just suggest an approximate figure?'

'It would be done with our commercial people, you understand, but...a ball-park figure...I suppose ten thousand pounds wouldn't be unusual, linked to various guarantees.'

'Ten thousand?' Patsy tried to keep the irritation out of her voice.

'Something along those lines.'

'This isn't working at all,' she said. 'Can we try another system? I mention a figure and you agree. Or not.'

He looked at her. 'It's not our usual approach, but...all right. If it helps to get the ball moving. What sort of figure did you have in mind, Mrs Bannister?'

'Ten million.'

From the beginning she'd planned to quote this sum; had actually practised it a few times in the bathroom mirror. Even so, producing the words in company sounded outlandish. Andy and the junior researcher took little intakes of breath but Roche seemed unmoved. He repeated the amount.

'You want ten million pounds?'

'That's it,' she said. 'I'm not greedy. If I involve the lawyers it'll be a lot more.'

He was stern and silent for a while, but she reckoned he was only pretending to ponder the proposal.

'I can see you know the value of research discoveries like this,' he said eventually.

'There's never been one like this, has there?' she countered.

'No there hasn't. You're talking about making people younger. Fantastic as it sounds, I'm willing to take the idea seriously. In a way, the figure you've mentioned reassures me about the validity of your claim.' He got to his feet. 'Look, Mrs Bannister, I don't think we can move this on much further today. There'll be an awful lot to sort out if we do go into partnership together. I'll talk to our commercial people and you'll need to get lawyers in, despite what you say. You'll hear from me very shortly, I promise.'

Essentially Roche's ponderous statement closed the meeting. Patsy left the Global Chemicals building and walked for a while beside the Thames. Normally the open landscape and the volume of water flowing past would have brought a sense of elation, but her spirits were unusually subdued. What's wrong girl? she asked herself. You're on the edge of ten million pounds. Could have been twenty if you'd pressed. She felt like someone caught up in a gold rush. The quest for lucre had overshadowed all her usual instincts. She sensed it happening but was powerless to resist.

*** *** ***

Carol felt the atmosphere immediately she let herself into the house that evening. Her mother and father were in different rooms but their mutual antipathy sent out icy vibrations. Jack was in the lounge staring at an empty TV screen.

He rose gamely to his feet. 'Carol - what a nice surprise.'

She kissed him. 'What's going on?'

'What do you mean?'

'Dad!' she said, exasperated. 'It's your daughter here, hello! You can cut the atmosphere with a knife. You've had a row, haven't you?'

Jack was silent.

'I'll take that as a "yes". Well, well - quite like the old days.'

'What d'you mean?' he said again.

'Have you really forgotten? I don't believe it. Come on, dad, what's it all about?'

'I couldn't begin to tell you, Carol,' he said heavily. 'We're not going to be good company, I'm afraid.'

She looked crestfallen. 'That casts a shadow over my news, then.'

'What news,' said Patsy, coming into the lounge and kissing her daughter. 'Would you like a cup of tea?'

'No thanks, mum. The temperature in here's too low for me.'

'And where's that bloke of yours? We still haven't seen him. I suppose it's all fallen through. Again.'

'Well you're wrong about that, clever clogs. He's very much around.

In fact he's given me something I've never had before.'

'How nice,' Patsy said. 'Something you've always wanted?'

'Not exactly, mum.' Carol gave her mother a meaningful glare. 'Something you've always wanted.'

Patsy stared at her, then sat down heavily on the sofa. 'Oh!' she said.

Carol knelt beside her. 'Is that all you can say? Oh! I thought you'd be pleased.'

Patsy gripped her daughter's hand but still said nothing. The most peculiar expression had subsumed her face. Her eyes were like a blind woman's.

'What is it, mum?' Carol said.

'Carol! Are you expecting, then?' Jack had belatedly woken up to the situation. 'Are you going to marry this man, or what?'

'Oh dad, people don't worry about marrying these days. We'll live together. We are living together. Maybe we'll marry, who knows? Who cares? Aren't you pleased either?'

'I'm sorry, love, of course I'm pleased. If you're happy, I am.'

'I'm...I'm so happy I can hardly breathe.'

'Then congratulations, dear. Come 'ere.'

When Jack had hugged her she turned back to her mother. 'And you, mum. A grandmother at last.'

There was a silence before Patsy said in a faint, distant voice, 'I suppose so.'

'What's the matter?' said Carol, sinking to her knees again.

'Oh, they don't have grandmothers in this brave new world of Patsy's,' Jack said. 'Nothing like that.'

'I'm lost here,' said Carol.

'Grandmothers will be mothers. Mothers'll be children.' Jack was shouting the words out with a bitterness unprecedented in his daughter's experience. 'The world'll be a sea of kids, Carol. Come to think of it, we won't need any new ones. You can throw yours back. The planet'll be full up. There'll be people on every inch of land. They'll be falling off the cliffs into the sea. Oh, it's going to be such fun.'

'Dad, what is it?' Never in her life had Carol heard such a speech from her father.

'It's all right, Carol.' Patsy had risen from the sofa, the distant stare banished. She looked and sounded like the old Patsy, capable and decisive. 'It might be best if you go just now. I need to talk to your father.'

'I don't want to leave you like this.'

'I know but it'll be all right, I promise. I'll fill you in later.'

'Well...'

'And congratulations, dear. I am pleased. I really am. You just took me back a bit. It's been a difficult week. You can't imagine how difficult. I'm really happy for you.'

In the ten years since she'd struck out on her own, Carol had never once been asked to leave her old home, but she took the hint and got out of her parents' way. Jack and Patsy heard the front door close, then Carol's car starting up on the porch. Then they heard her get out of the car and call out. Her words carried clearly: 'What are you doing there? Who are you?'

Jack hurried through the back door with Patsy close behind him. Carol's engine was running, and the car's headlights illuminated a swathe of the garden.

'Are you all right?' he said.

'I'm fine, dad.' Her voice was tense but not scared. 'There's someone down there. I had my headlights on and caught him in the glare. I think he went behind the shed.'

In the headlights' full beam every bloom in Patsy's garden seemed to stand out sharply, every blade of grass on the lawn. Jack advanced towards the shed, feeling surprisingly calm.

'All right, come on out,' he called.

'Be careful, Jack,' said Patsy.

'Come out and walk towards the house,' Jack called.

A figure detached itself from behind the shed and began walking towards him; a tall, middle-aged figure moving with almost impertinent calmness. The last thing he looked like was a criminal.

'Look out dad, there's something in his hand,' Carol called.

'It's not a knife, is it,' said Patsy.

'No, no,' Jack said. 'It's a torch. Here he comes.' He raised his voice again. 'All right mate, what are you doing in our garden?'

But Patsy forestalled the answer. 'Mr Roche!' she cried.

'Good evening, Mrs Bannister,' called Roche.

Jack turned in astonishment. 'You know this man?'

'I do,' she said, running forward to him. 'Leave this to me.'

'I don't know about that.'

She put a hand on his arm and lowered her voice to a whisper. 'Jack, I can sort this out, I promise. I'll sort everything out. And I mean everything. Will you trust me? You always have, and you can again. Please?'

He only hesitated for a moment. 'All right. What do you want me to do?'

'Go back by the kitchen door, out of the headlights. You too, Carol.'

Baffled, father and daughter retreated from the glare, and Patsy went forward to meet the man on her own.

'I'm sorry about this, Mrs Bannister,' Roche said.

'You should be,' she said. 'What was it you said? "That's not the way Global Chemicals operates". Well, we know better now, don't we. I ought to call the police.'

He looked dreadfully embarrassed, standing exposed in the light. 'I hope you won't do that,' he said. 'We wanted to be sure. We needed proof.'

'Oh yes. And did you find what you wanted, Mr Roche?'

'I didn't. Look, whatever I'd found, or didn't find, it wouldn't affect the terms of any agreement.'

'There won't be an agreement,' Patsy said.

'Please don't be hasty, Mrs Bannister.'

'It's not that I don't want to cooperate with Global Chemicals - though I don't. There won't be an agreement because there isn't a discovery. I lied to you. Go back and tell that to your bosses. I've had plastic surgery, and loads of it.'

'What's she on about?' Carol asked her father on the back door step. 'She's lost the plot completely.'

'Let your mum talk, love,' Jack told her. 'She's doing all right.'

'But your claim, Mrs Bannister,' Roche was saying. 'What was all that about?'

'I lied,' Patsy said. 'I'm a sad old woman, surely you can see that. It was a hoax, and you fell for it.'

Roche looked uncertain. 'You were very convincing.'

'Oh, I'm good. It's not the first time, you see.'

Roche hesitated. 'I don't know...'

'You're welcome to come back tomorrow in the daytime - have a really good look around.'

'As a matter of fact, I've been here a while,' Roche said. 'There's nothing unusual.'

'I mean ask yourself, Mr Roche,' Patsy said. 'Was it ever remotely possible?'

When he spoke again, Roche's voice was heavy with regret. 'No. No, I don't suppose it was. It was a dream.' He stood head bowed, chasing the dream away. Patsy saw the plans he'd constructed, the visions of a lifetime, draining out of him. She knew how he felt. He gave a last, lingering look round the garden. 'Well, I'd better be on my way. Thank you for your forbearance, Mrs Bannister. I'm sorry it's ended like this.'

With a little nod towards Jack and Carol he walked away.

Patsy watched him go, then joined her husband at the back door. 'I'm sorry, Jack,' she said. 'I've been off my head, haven't I? It took Carol's news to bring me to my senses. I'm so sorry. Please forgive me.'

Jack reached out an arm and drew her to him. 'All right now,' he said.

He held his wife close and kissed her. She kissed him back. He went on kissing.

'Hey, you two,' Carol said. 'Steady on.'

Jack looked up at her. 'How would you feel about a little uncle or aunt for your baby, Carol?' and before she had time to answer, 'Only kidding'.

'Would someone mind telling me what's going on,' Carol said.

At the same moment Jack and Patsy reached out and drew her into their embrace.

'You really don't want to go there,' Jack said.

*** *** ***

The next day Jack visited the allotment carrying an unfamiliar implement. When Stan arrived shortly afterwards he found Jack hacking at the base of the pod tree with an axe.

''Ello, 'ello,' said Stan, 'Are my old eyes deceiving me?'

'Morning, Stan,' said Jack, breathing heavily.

'You're working up a lather there, Jack me lad.'

'Nearly done.' Jack drew a shirt-sleeve across his brow. 'I'm feeling my age this morning, Stanley. Tell you the truth, I've never chopped down a tree before. Don't really know what I'm doing.'

'I can see that,' said Stan. 'Which way is it supposed to fall?'

'I thought, across your cucumbers.'

'Nice. I'm sorry it's come to this, Jack.'

'Sorry? Why, you old humbug.'

'No, straight up, I'm gonna miss the old tree,' Stan said. 'Nice bit of shade on an 'ot day. Somefing a bit different in the allotment.'

'You old rogue. You've done nothing but complain ever since it arrived.'

'Only kidding. I've nuffin' against the thing.'

'Well I have. Stanley, you cannot begin to imagine the trouble this tree has caused.'

As they stood gossiping, a powerful gust of wind blew across the allotments. The pod tree swayed, creaked, and began to fall - in the wrong direction. Stan stood and watched as the top of it went neatly through a small green-house that stood on the edge of his land. There was a crash of breaking glass, then silence.

'You missed the cucumbers, any road,' said Stan.

Jack was overcome with embarrassment. 'I'm so sorry, Stan. What an idiot I am. I'll pay for a replacement, of course. I am sorry.'

'Don't worry, mate.' Stan was unperturbed.

'I do worry. I'm awfully sorry.'

'It was ancient, that greenhouse,' Stan insisted. 'Had it since our ruby wedding anniversary. No sweat. After all, Jack me lad, nuffin' lasts for ever, does it?

~ Invasion ~

It started on a Saturday evening, as Vince sat on his balcony gazing at the market garden. The muezzin was calling from the mosque down the road, but a different sound reached him too, a slight clink of crockery from the direction of his kitchen. He rose and strolled along the corridor to check. Nobody there. Curiously, the piece of steak he'd taken out to de-freeze was sitting on the worktop a few inches from its plate.

Normally Ragah would have cooked, but he'd sent her home. She'd arrived for work that morning with an arm swathed in stained bandages. A gas cylinder had exploded in her home and created carnage. She should have stayed in bed; not for the first time Vince was amazed at the woman's toughness. He told her not to come back for a few days - with reluctance. Ragah's cooking was only just edible but anything seemed better than doing it himself.

Surely he'd left that steak on the plate, hadn't he?

Vince replaced the meat and this time covered it with a colander. Back on the balcony, he sat watching dusk hit the garden. It came down quickly, as in all hot places. This was Vince's best moment of the day. The garden area – the size of a football pitch – was fading in the gloom; palm trees, fruit trees, the whole shoot of allah-knew-what shrubs and crops, indistinguishable one from the other. The men in *galabeahs* moved through the dusty greenery; not quickly – this was Egypt – but with serene, measured tread, as if markets and balance sheets had no place in the world. As Vince sat on his darkening balcony the day's heat ebbed away.

He'd only taken the flat because of the garden. Otherwise the place wasn't up to much. The big front reception room looked out on a main road and had only been used once. It had a chandelier. His landlord, who lived below, had told Vince about chandelier culture; when you married, the bride's family had to approve the size of the one you provided.

The second sign of invasion – after the self-motivating steak – came a few nights later when Vince was with his girlfriend. They were screwing in his narrow double bed with the shutters open onto the garden. The moon was out. At a crucial moment Rachel lifted her head and gazed at the wardrobe door.

'Look!'

Vince didn't want to look. He was inside the girl and it felt great. Bloody women, he thought; *whatever* they were up to – always ready for some diversion.

'Do look, Vince.'

He groaned, and followed her gaze. The iron railing that ran along the balcony was reflected by moonlight onto his wardrobe door. Above this was another reflection: the magnified, magic-lantern form of a mouse. Yes, a mouse. It gambolled on the rail like something from a Walt Disney movie.

'Whoops!'

This was Rachel registering the deflation of her partner's erection. Vince had gone as flat as a pancake. Who could compete with a gambolling mouse? He bounded from the bed followed by a shriek of Rachel laughter, and tip-toed onto the balcony. For a moment the mouse eluded him, until he saw its averted head peering up from a window box. The rodent was motionless, presumably frozen in fear. Then Vince moved and it scuttled away down the side of the house.

'Hmm.' Vince went back to bed. 'Strange.'

'A friend of yours?'

'Not now he isn't. Little bugger. He's interrupted the act of love.'

'Now then, Vince – don't use big words you don't understand.'

He rolled across the mattress, but she shrank from him in mock alarm. Apparently their little moment was over. He'd noticed before how a tiny incident could turn a woman's mood. How changeable they were. Just because he'd used the 'l' word.

They'd met when he cut open his hand on the building site, and was taken to the hospital where Rachel worked as a nurse. He'd invited her to go riding by the pyramids, and they started seeing each other. He liked having her around in the evening because she turned him on. That sort of slim body and white skin had always been his thing. In the mornings, though, rushing a pre-work breakfast with coffee and rolls, and Egyptian jam – well, the magic had pretty well dissipated by then.

All the same...

Damn that mouse!

As it happened Rachel was present at the next manifestation too. She was sitting on one of his two toilets when a rat appeared at the bottom of the porcelain and tried to jump up. Rachel pulled the chain and washed it away, characteristically unfussed about the incident; but then – as Vince pointed out – she didn't have any dangly bits to assault.

She wasn't there a day later when Vince found a mouse in the bath. He beat it senseless with a rolled up towel and threw the body out of the window.

Twice stretched the boundaries of coincidence. But three times?

Cairo was the problem, or so he told himself. He'd never liked the place. He hated the traffic, so clogged that the shortest journey took half an hour. The old cars in the streets left behind a miasma of exhaust fumes. There was an array of more medieval vehicles still. That morning he'd seen a horse-drawn cart full of bones and a cloud of flies in pursuit. Driving was a nightmare. You swerved to avoid a goat and ran into an open man-hole.

He'd seized on the garden view to get away from all that. It really did help if he could sit on his balcony for long enough, just looking. The calm spread through his body like a dose of morphia. For a time Cairo receded: the filth of the streets; the fumes; that dead horse out in the desert.

Soon enough the worlds outside and inside were going to meet. It had happened in this building, when sewage welled up to fill his landlord's basement. Now the rodents. Vince dreamt of death and decay. During the night he could feel his own blood beating a tattoo on the pillow.

At work that day a friend had brought in a grotesque face-mask she'd got in Paris. Vince put it on and went off to wind up his boss. Descending a staircase he passed one of the secretaries and noted through the eye-holes how she shrank away from him, pressing her body against the wall.

He went to the *suq* in search of mouse-traps and they sold him a cage. You put food inside on a lever connected to the propped-open door. When something disturbed the bait the door slammed shut. He woke next morning to find two large rats inside, both looking utterly dispirited. Vince poked a stick through the bars, and the larger one turned its head away. Getting rid of these unwanted visitors posed a problem. In the end he filled the sink with water and drowned them.

Still they came in, on a daily basis. He began to think in terms of a biblical plague, with rodents taking the place of locusts. The suddenness of the influx struck him as sinister. Why now? Why all at once? Why in *his* place? He checked with the Egyptian landlord, but there'd been no incidents on the floor below.

The fourteenth rodent – he kept a record – appeared when Rachel was again in the flat. They were on the sofa when a rat came from the balcony and scurried across the room. Rachel leapt up to give chase.

'Come on, Vince.'

They followed down the corridor and into the kitchen. Vince stared around at the small space.

'Where is the little bugger?'

'It's all right – we've got him.' She pointed at a ground-level cupboard with the door ajar. 'It went in there.'

'Right!' Vince dragged the giant waste bin across the floor, aiming its mouth at the cupboard door. 'Pull the door right back.'

She did so. Nothing. They peered at the two empty cupboard shelves.

'I'm sure it went in there,' said Rachel.

Vince knelt and shoved his head into the cupboard. As he did so something flew past his right ear to land in the waste bin.

'Christ!' he said.

He seized the broom and stabbed with its handle, but only got glancing blows. They could hear the rat crashing about the bottom of the bin.

'Downstairs,' Vince cried.

They ran down to the street with bin and broom. At least the traffic had gone at this late hour. The blank-faced buildings lined up either side of the road. Vince stabbed again with the broom handle. He thought it hit something soft but couldn't see in the darkness. Rachel picked up a heavy rock from the central reservation.

'I'll get the little sod. Turn the bin over.'

'Be careful,' said Vince, doing as she said.

It was strange to see a rat limping. The thing had lurched a yard down the road before Rachel brought the rock down. That did the trick. The vile tail quivered and was still.

'Thanks, Rache,' Vince said. 'You were great.'

He meant it. She was flushed with the chase, lithe in skin-tight jeans. God, she looked terrific. He must see her more, make a thing of it.

'OK then.' She dusted her hands one against the other. 'Nice way to round things off.'

'Whad'you mean?'

'It's been fine, Vince. I've enjoyed it. And to tell the truth, I really like your cock up me. But...well, you know...'

He didn't know. 'Rachel!'

She took a step forward, kissed him quickly. 'Tra-ra, then. I won't say "Be seeing you".'

'*Rachel.*'

He stood and watched as she marched down the road towards the Nile.

The fourteenth rodent was the last. Vince never knew why the invasion ended so suddenly. He had a vague theory about the last one having been taken outside, back where it came from, breaking the cycle. Crazy thoughts like that. Anyway it was over.

Life went back to a sort of normal, but he found it hard to concentrate at work. He missed Rachel now she'd gone, more than he used to miss her absences. Her replacement - Judy from the embassy shop - was a sad disappointment.

The worst thing about the invasion was the way it spoiled the market garden. He still sat out on the balcony but it wasn't the same. That view – the one that had kept him sane – he now imagined teeming with little forms sporting teeth and grotesque, snappy tails. Vince became rather strange about the whole affair. He had odd dreams, including one where Rachel was carried away on a tide of mice. His work suffered. Twice the boss took him aside to express concern. The embassy medic put him on anti-depressants.

A few months after the invasion Vince was encouraged to leave Cairo and return to Chelmsford. He met an Essex girl. Let us draw a veil...

~ Champagne reunion ~

It wasn't the first reunion of the year. I seemed to have reached the age when people reconnected with former colleagues, before sloping away to health-care and pallbearers. This particular group met as the official enquiry into phone hacking got under way. Rupert Murdoch was dissembling on all the media outlets and politicians fell over each other to tell the biggest lies.

The eight of us gathered at the champagne bar in St Pancras station. Britain was in recession, but long rows of tables were crammed with people drinking from the distinctive slim glasses at £10 a throw.

'David!' Adrian advanced towards me, an inflexion of surprise in his voice, as it always was at hand-shake time. 'Come and imbibe. They've put us on this table right at the end – apparently we're too disgraceful to be seen.'

I had no trouble over recognition, though he'd become quite portly in the 20 years since I'd seen him (or any of them). The reunion had been Adrian's idea, and he was much in evidence at our table, greeting arrivals and embarking on the sort of anecdotes that were so familiar to me. He was much the most successful member of our tribe in the organisation, and deservedly so.

We'd arranged to decant from the champagne bar into Searcy's restaurant, but even after we did so, one of our number was missing. Katie eventually arrived as we were placing the orders. She went round the table greeting people awkwardly from behind.

'Hello David.'

'What happened to you?'

'Too complicated to go into.'

In my vague memory of her, she used to come to work wearing scruffy black leggings, but she had on a decent dress this evening. All the same she looked different from the others. Adrian was in a suit, of course, and the women amongst us – all pushing 60 or beyond it – looked terrific. (As I approached the extremes of antiquity, my image of ideal womanhood was advancing upwards.) I suppose Katie was in her mid-50s, but she seemed...well, 'worn' was the only word. A strange scent as she kissed my ear put me in mind of moth-balls.

I sat opposite her, but it was hard to communicate in the rowdy restaurant. She spoke rarely, and then in a low voice. I wondered why she'd come at all. I talked instead to Suzie, partner of a civilised former colleague who was out of range down the table. As the only spouse present, Suzie was largely unknown to the rest of us.

'I'm an interloper,' were her opening words.

'Not at all,' I told her. 'You're here to prevent us from disappearing up our own fundaments.' (It was too soon to use the other word.)

Not that Suzie needed prior acquaintance to hold her own in conversation. She was another one like Adrian, still working full-time (an agency to do with asylum seekers), and it showed. She was personable, well-informed in all sorts of areas, and avid for all the extra intelligence she could get. I noticed her eyes drift away as she tried to take in conversations around the table. It was years since I'd been in that sort of company.

The contrast between workers and retirees was a theme of the evening. Those not in work had abandoned a pretence of 'keeping up' and retreated into personal obsessions; they were more self-absorbed, more eccentric, and on the whole more interesting.

A girl on the staff asked if we were happy with the food, an utterly dispassionate enquiry. It was a place where you would neither complain nor wax lyrical. I might have demurred at the choice of media channels though. They had a flat TV screen on the wall with subtitles for sound. Murdoch's face was absent for once, only to be supplanted by a banker justifying his billion-pound bonus.

We'd reached a natural break after the starter course. I grinned at Katie, who'd remained a virtual onlooker, and asked her to tell me what she'd been doing for the past 20 years.

'I've been working on aid projects in Africa. Nigeria, then southern Sudan.'

I'd never been one of the 'old Africa hands', but I'd known a few. They tended to piss in their garden after dinner, when there was a perfectly good toilet nearby. But Nigeria...! I'd been there all right, and vowed never to return. Colleagues had only accepted Lagos posts on promotion. As for south Sudan – well, I read the newspapers, like everyone else.

'Tell me about Sudan then. How long have you been there? Isn't it dangerous?'

'Three years.' Katie spoke without animation. I had to lean across the table to catch her words. 'It's not at all dangerous on the southern border. We work with the black Christians there.'

I'd assumed she was employed by the Overseas Development Administration, who'd been such obstreperous partners, but...

'David, the ODA changed its name years ago,' she told me. 'No, I'm with American aid. It's easier as long as you follow the rule book. They don't keep chopping and changing. But as a British woman...you have to be twice as good as the American staff to survive.'

'What do you miss most, working out there?'

'I miss the seasons. The Sudan is virtually the same all year round. Dusk comes at seven every day.

It was cool inside the restaurant and Katie pulled a jacket around her shoulders. 'I bet you don't need that in Sudan,' I said.

'Er, no.'

'What sort of temperatures do you get?'

'It's 40 degrees at the moment.'

'Bloody hell.' I might just have tolerated that in my 20s, but never at

Katie's age. 'I suppose it's cooler at night.'

'Hardly.'

'But you have air-conditioning.'

'Not really. We sleep outside – that helps a bit.'

She'd made no attempt to dramatise her situation, or for that matter to talk about it at all. Details had to be dragged out of her. But I was hooked now and I persisted. I told her I'd read about Gertrude Bell in Baghdad, and the problems she'd had sleeping in similar temperatures early in the 20th century.

'As I recall, Bell used to soak a sheet in cold water and hang it up beside her bed. For as long as it took to dry, she got some relief from the heat and was able to snatch some sleep.'

Katie nodded. 'Sleep is a real problem. I don't do that, but I soak a sheet and wrap it round me. Has the same sort of effect.'

I stole a look at her, genuinely astonished. Small wonder she looked so worn beside the rest of us. Again I struggled to comprehend her. Why had she come here tonight? To spend a few hours among the fleshpots? To remind herself of the comfortable existence she'd left behind? I had no idea what was going on in her head.

The restaurant was packed now. Diners brayed across the tables, scarcely aware of the food and drink going down their throats. The din from the champagne bar still drifted in from outside.

'I don't know how you do it,' I told her. 'What made you take on this gruelling life?' I stopped myself from adding 'at your age'.

'Obstinacy?' She raised an eyebrow – as near as she came to humour.

'Is that it?'

'I'm interested. I'm quite good at it.'

'Understated' didn't begin to describe her. She'd not been seen as a high flier 20 years earlier, far from it; I'd had trouble remembering her at all. Now I felt humbled by her.

'I think you're heroic,' I blurted out.

She broke off a piece of bread and chewed. 'What have you been up to?' she said, without much interest.

~Second home ~

Luke parked the car and walked the few yards to the block of flats. He paused at the entrance to give the place the once-over. It was as he'd imagined, only worse: uglier, more dilapidated, *darker*. He could see the first flight of stairs, with a damp mark running down them where someone had casually dragged a wet mop; some cowboy agents, acting for absentee landlords. He felt profoundly grateful to be just passing through. Clear out the contents – hire a skip, maybe – get a furniture removal firm; a day or two at most, which was all he could spare anyway. He wouldn't be mooning about over artefacts from the past – not bloody likely.

A woman emerged from a ground floor flat with a toddler in a push-chair. She looked thoroughly pissed-off about something. He moved to let her pass, but she stopped and gave him a glare.

'What do you want?'

He stared back. 'I'm visiting my father's flat – on the second floor.'

'Oh that. I've not seen you here before.'

'I've not been here before.' She looked just the type to monitor what went on in the block. The toddler started to whine, and she gave the push-chair a shake. 'Your father's not there anyway.'

'I know,' said Luke. 'He's dead.'

Without a word the woman moved off, thrusting the push-chair before her with a passion.

Luke entered the block and mounted the stairs. For a bloke of 50 he still moved about with commendable briskness, but his footsteps slowed as he neared the second floor. He really did not want to do this. With reluctance he fished out the old-fashioned key Frances had given him and unlocked the door marked '8'. It pushed open against a tide of circulars on the mat.

The door of the flat behind him flew open and a voice burst out.

'At last. I wondered what on earth...'

The woman broke off with a little squeak of 'oh'. She was round-faced, dressed in heavy and (he thought) expensive clothes. She moved with difficulty yet was strangely buoyant for someone in...what...her 60s, at least.

'I'm so sorry,' she said. 'I...I thought it had to be Reg.'

'It's OK,' he told her, wondering.

She peered, on the dark landing, and gasped 'You're Luke?'

'That's right. But how...'

'I'm sorry.' Her hands fluttered. 'You've never come before.'

'No.'

Luke wasn't known for being perceptive — both wives had made that clear – but he saw one thing; this woman was making a big effort to hold back questions.

'I'm sorry,' she said for a third time. She took a step back into her flat, stumbled and almost fell. He sprang forward and held her in both arms.

'Let me help.'

'I'll be OK.' She held onto the door jamb. Then the question came. 'Is anything wrong? Is Reg ill?'

'Can I help you to a chair?'

'I'm all right, really. If you could just tell me.'

There was nothing else for it. 'I'm afraid my father died.'

She stared with dead eyes. 'I knew as soon as I saw you.'

'Can I do anything?'

'Nothing. I don't exist.'

'Please.'

She touched his arm. 'I'm all right now. Thank you, Luke. It's fine, really.'

She backed into her flat pulling the door to, and he let her. He stood on the dark landing for a moment, then entered 'no. 8', closed the door, and stood with his back to it staring into the lounge. In the gloom – the curtains were pulled across – he could just see into the bathroom and what he took to be a small bedroom. In one corner of the lounge a

Belling stove and a sink stood in for a kitchen. The flat reminded Luke of the bed-sitter he'd taken after first leaving home. No place for a man in his late 70s.

What the hell was he doing here?, he asked himself At the wake following the funeral Frances had dangled the key in front of him. 'I know you're awfully busy,' she told him, 'But will you do one thing for me? It's that flat – I can't face it. I'm sorry to ask, Luke. You and I haven't been close, I know. In fact I wonder if I'll ever see you again.'

He'd known about the flat but had never given it a thought. When his parents divorced, his father had got in touch with Frances, an old dancing partner, and it wasn't all that long before he'd moved into her home. With the caution of middle-age Frances had wanted a safety valve; maybe his father had too. Whatever...the old man hung onto the flat he'd been living in and spent every Monday there, giving them a break from each other. The routine was unusual but seemed to work. Routine became ritual. By all accounts they'd not missed a Monday apart in years.

Luke crossed the lounge to draw the curtains, then wished he hadn't. The little room was vestigially furnished: a small table, an armchair, two upright chairs and a TV set. On the far side a motorbike had been taken apart, the pieces laid on newspaper covering the floor. Dirty plates were piled on the sink. There was no reading material in sight beyond a copy of the *Racing post*. Luke recognised his father's spoor all right; infinite trouble with machines ('I can get anything to work, my boy'), but washing-up, no.

The phone call from Frances – the one that broke the news – interrupted a big meeting at work. Luke had been preoccupied. He'd not felt much beyond the frozen emotions his father always inspired. Now in this room a great lowering of spirits descended. Still nothing personal, just the discouraging scene; the trappings of a life-end, maybe a premonition of his own.

He willed himself to enter the other room. The duvet was half on, half off the bed, tangled up with an old sweater that Luke recognised from way back. Otherwise the place was as spartan as a monk's cell. Bed aside, the only furniture was a tallboy; the door hung open revealing trousers on a hanger. Luke idly opened the top drawer expecting to find nothing. Instead – he actually took a pace back – the drawer was half full of letters, dozens of them, scattered about higgledy piggledy. And recent letters, by the look of them. What the fuck? They were by far the most interesting thing in the flat – the *only* interesting thing. Who could possibly...?

He recoiled from the thought of probing his father's personal life, but in the event it wasn't necessary. One letter lay open at the signature: 'With all my love, Julie'. Julie! Julie who?

Standing there staring into the drawer, Luke realised someone was knocking on the door; probably had been knocking for a while. He strode across to open it. The woman from across the landing, leaning on a stick.

'I'm really sorry to disturb you.'

'It's OK,' he said. 'I don't mind being disturbed, actually.'

'It took me by surprise, seeing you there. I wasn't thinking straight. Then I realised...I mean, even my fuddled brain...you'll be clearing the place out. You're bound to come across things.'

Luke started at her. 'Julie?'

'That's me,' she said, with a show of spirit.

'I didn't read anything,' he said quickly. 'One letter was open at the name.'

'It's all right.'

She didn't move, so he made a decision. 'Look, will you come in for a bit?'

'Are you sure about that?'

'Come on. I might even be able to lay my hands on some tea.'

'If you're sure. Thank you.' She made her way in, moving painfully. 'I can find the tea. It'll be powdered milk though.'

He grinned. 'Anything.'

'And Reg always had digestive biscuits on the go.'

'Oh yes – he would do.' Luke said it to show her he knew *something* about his father; this woman who seemed to know more than he did. He remembered the biscuit tin from home 40 years back; it's exact position on the kitchen shelf.

'I'm sorry.' (She was always saying 'sorry'.) It's all right, isn't it...my knowing where the biscuits are?'

It embarrassed him that she'd read his thoughts. 'Don't be daft.'

'Shall I help you assemble the motorbike too?'

They both laughed, and the atmosphere lightened a bit. She showed him where to find tea, and biscuits. A few minutes later they were sitting on the upright chairs, facing across the table.

'I want to tell you about it,' she said.

'Julie, you don't have to tell me anything.'

'I'd like to, if you don't mind. Because of...you know, the circumstances, I've couldn't tell anyone. It would be a relief to talk.' She'd been crying, he could see, but for the time being seemed almost ebullient. 'And anyway, there's another reason.'

'What do you mean?'

'I'll come to that. You'll have gathered...so many letters...your father and I had become close friends.' Luke put a mental question-mark after 'friends' but she was ahead of him again. 'Well, more than friends, of course. And yes, we tried that too – you'd be surprised what a couple of arthritic old codgers can get up to...'

'Honestly, Julie, you don't...'

'Bereavement is a truth drug,, isn't it. And love – that's another one. We were better at kissing and cuddling, really – like Elvis Presley used to be – that's what they say.'

'Please.' He raised a hand, as if to ward her off. 'I can't get my head round it.'

Again she anticipated him. 'You'll be thinking – what did washed-out old Reg have to offer a woman. I feel privileged to have known him. I've been so happy since he rolled up on the doorstep. A corner of someone's life...it can be better than the full-on stuff.'

'You keep reading my thoughts.'

'Sorry. I've been accused of that before. It's west country people – we all think we've got second sight. What I mean is...your father and I owed each other nothing.' Quirky she might be, but the woman expressed herself with delicate precision. 'No financial commitments. Simple affection. I expect you think I'm ridiculously romantic.'

'It's quite refreshing, actually,' Luke said sincerely. 'I come from the business world.'

'I'm sorry I missed the funeral, but I'd always known...I mean they wouldn't want me drifting in like the ghost of Macbeth...people choking on their vol-au-vents.'

'Nobody knew about you, I'm sure of that.'

'I hope not. He wanted to tell *you* though.'

'*Me*!'

'Are you surprised?'

'I'd be the last person.'

'*No*.' She'd spoken forcefully, then looked embarrassed. 'I'm sorry...I've no right.'

'What did you mean?'

Still the thoughts came out in ordered fashion. 'I don't know you, of course. But I suppose coming here...finding this little world...it's like a journey of discovery.'

'What's your point?'

Footsteps scraped on the stairwell. The letter-box flapped and another circular fluttered onto the door-mat. Luke tried to collect his thoughts. He felt uneasy without knowing why. Despite the drawn curtains the room was dark, and utterly silent – like a place the world had overlooked. A faint smell of grease came from the dismantled bits of motorbike. The woman sat composed across the table, waiting. He thought he could see the attraction to his father. Which was odd because her fey personality was streets away from his own. He should have been drawn to Frances – another from the murky world of business – yet had never got on with her.

The woman started up again, like a tape-recorder set in motion. 'It's just that...Reg passed on his thoughts. *All* of them, I think. And I did too. I'd never believed two people could do that.'

'Me neither.'

'And if I've got this right, he wasn't always like that with you.'

'Are you kidding! If he really told you his thoughts, you'll know.' Bitterness welled up, like a metallic taste in the mouth. 'Something about me – I don't know what – really turned him off.'

'*No.*'

Again that forceful negative. Luke felt irritation growing. This bloody woman. She'd coaxed a revelation from him – not his style at all – and now she was laying down the law. 'You can't possibly know,' he broke out.

'I'm sorry. I'm only passing on what he told me.' She continued as he sat fulminating. 'I never had children, so I've hardly a right to comment. Looking on from outside...' - god, how her quiet, tenacious tone was getting up his nose - 'I sometimes think a father and son are ambivalent about the qualities they have in common. Does that make any sense?'

'It sounds like Mickey Mouse Freud to me.'

'Have you found the scrapbook?'

'Scrapbook! That's hardly like my father.'

'No – you can't oil a scrapbook, can you? I thought it would be with the letters.'

'Just a moment.' He stood abruptly and went into the bedroom, eyeing the bed with distaste. *She'd* have been on it. *She'd* have been with him under the duvet. In the bottom drawer of the tallboy he found a thick, spiral-bound album. He flipped back the cover and saw three photos of himself, aged almost nothing.

Luke returned to the lounge and put it on the table. She sat silent as he leafed through the pages. Some of the early snaps he remembered, but the further he went into his life – the sequence was chronological – the less he understood: school reports, then photos of the graduation ceremony at uni (which his father had missed); pictures with both his wives (where had his father got hold of them?); scraps of his handwriting on meaningless notes (one read 'Dad, Sorry I can't make it Wednesday – hope you understand'); loads of press cuttings about the business, from local and national papers; photocopies of the two awards; much more.

He closed the book, shaking his head.

'You've not seen this?' she said.

'No way. I don't understand.'

After a moment she said 'He told me you used to get on, at one time.'

'When I was young, yes. Later it fell apart. I didn't like the way he treated my mother. Then there was a big row about money, and he started to favour my brother. It just...happened. Then when my mother died...we've hardly spoken in years. He just turned against me.'

'He adored you.'

The simple statement confirmed the other stuff; there was no gainsaying it. The barriers fell and emotion raced to make up lost time. The scrapbook lay open and his tears fell on a photograph of himself accepting an award. They went on and on though he tried to stop.

'Stupid,' he mumbled.

She reached out to put a hand over his, but he shook her off.

He stared, and of course she divined what he was thinking and stumbled to her feet. 'I thought you'd want to know.'

He escorted her to the door, refusing to make eye-contact. He knew what the bloody woman wanted. (Oh yes, Julie, two can play at mind-reading.) To stay in touch would have given her love a toe-hold. It wasn't going to happen. The least he could do was stop that. What she'd had he could have had. That he was to blame only hardened his resolution.

'The place will be cleared out within a week,' he said. 'I'll drop the letters back through your letter-box.' He left her standing on the landing and closed the door.

~ Goodbye, son ~

Rogers entered the restaurant and was led to a place in the corner. He passed a bearded Englishman sitting at another table and gave a minimal nod of recognition. The man had been on the same flight out; an irrigation engineer, if memory served, no doubt involved in some lucrative project or other. You'd need a bloody good reason to come to this dump of a country, Rogers thought. Money was the only conceivable motive he could come up with, and it wasn't nearly good enough.

He tried to check his watch but the restaurant's lighting was almost non-existent. Lagos fashion obviously decreed a dark ambience in its eating places. The room was an array of ghostly heads-and-shoulders floating over white table cloths. He inclined his wrist towards the lighted candle next to his place setting. 6pm. Forty-five minutes to eat, half an hour, say, for a taxi to the airport. Plenty of time to negotiate his way through the terminal's notorious check-out rituals. If they were anything like those on arrival he had an uncomfortable time of it ahead. He felt a faint frisson of panic in case there were problems about getting away.

Rogers had knocked about in some undesirable parts of the world, but not seen anything like Lagos. His Personnel Department found it almost impossible to fill posts there; people had to be promoted into them. As each day of his stay went by he saw more clearly why that was. He remembered how, after the flight in, the short-term visitors from Britain - men on their own - had herded together in the baggage hall shouting bravado comments to no-one in particular - 'Here we go again, lads'; 'Watch your backs'; 'Manyana, manyana' - and Rogers had realised with a shock that they were scared, were shouting to keep their spirits up. It started at the airport, where a Nigerian security guard had detained him for no apparent reason; you needed a bribe to get out of the place! He'd spent the week at a woman colleague's flat, in a compound set aside for diplomats and businessmen. A whole community of poor Nigerians lived on the rough ground outside the gates. His taxi had had to drive round one of them, a large black woman squatting in the road to piss. Rogers's colleague was a robust girl, not easily fazed. He found her with a nasty bruise on the arm, a souvenir from being robbed that afternoon in a park. 'The guy had my money,' she said phlegmatically. 'He just hit me for fun.' The whole week Rogers was there she had no water supply. They filled her kettle from the compound swimming pool and went to a colleague's house for showers.

He finished the restaurant meal earlier than intended. There was nothing for it but to summon the bill and get moving. You paid at a cash register near the door, and he joined a small queue there. Ahead of him were two people with 'English' written all over them: a grizzled, middle-aged bloke and a boy about sixteen.

'This won't take long,' the older bloke told him. 'Visitor to Lagos?'

'How did you know?'

'When you've been here as long as I have,' the man said cheerfully,

'Any expat you don't know is a visitor.'

'Actually I'm on my way out. I go from here to the airport.'

'No kidding! Us too. Tim here's back to the UK after his holidays.' The man swung round and took Rogers's hand in a horny grip. 'Bill Bates. And my son, Tim. Look, come along with us. It helps to have someone show you the ropes. I've got a Range Rover outside.'

Rogers hesitated. It would be a godsend to be 'shown the ropes' at the wretched airport, but he didn't want to intrude on a delicate goodbye scene between father and son. 'It's kind of you, but I can easily get a taxi,' he said without conviction.

'Nonsense.' Bates was insistent. 'You come along.'

Soon the Range Rover was bowling along the airport road, cases shoved in the boot. Rogers had the back seat to himself. The darkness and the easy motion of the vehicle induced a mood of reflection. He'd met Bates and his kind in many outposts of old empire - technical consultants and advisers who could make things work better than the locals, but would never hold the posts of consequence. Their wives had had enough and were back in the UK, separated or divorced more often than not. The men scratched a fortnightly letter home, drank heavily in the British club, watched the previous month's football matches sent out on video. Mostly they worked. Work was a habit and a need. It was better in places like this where management theory was only in textbooks and the owner's nephew was nominally in charge. Even the labyrinth of local allegiances was obscurely enjoyable to negotiate.

They put up with the heat and loneliness, and the shortage of spares.

He heard Bates curse and there was a brief explosion of light as a car passed them on full headlights, horn blaring. Rogers stirred from his reverie. Bates had scarcely said a word at the wheel but his son now made an observation about 'mum' followed by a word which sounded like 'birthday'. Whatever it was caused consternation. Bates raised his eyes skywards, said a drawn-out 'sugar', as though the son were still at kindergarten, then gave vent to a 'bugger. Then the son said 'Dad, why don't I...' something or other, and Bates weighed in with a grateful 'Could you really, Tim?'. He rummaged under the dashboard and started writing on a slip of paper, still doing 60 down the highway. It was Lagos, after all.

'Saved my life, Tim,' Bates murmured, handing over the slip of paper. 'Slip that under the wrapping. Get her something nice - you'll know. I'll write a cheque before you leave.'

It sounded as if Bates still had a wife, at least, though distanced from her by an ocean and half of Africa. Rogers guessed he was enjoying the collusion over the birthday present. Until then conversation had sounded forced, as if he and the son were acquaintances rather than flesh and blood. Suddenly it was clear why Bates had been content to have a stranger along. It helped him to gloss over this awkward parting from a son he'd lost touch with. The boy had come out to visit, sure enough, but they must have seen little of each other in recent years. Rogers could almost feel the pain under the man's bluff manner. This wasn't a relationship that could be negotiated - not like one with a difficult customer, or a works manager out to make trouble. This was close to the bone. This was the cut of commitment in Bates's solitary self-sufficiency.

'Only ten minutes more, Michael.' Despite his own preoccupations, Bates had remembered to keep the back-seat passenger happy. 'Then we'll have arrived...at the travellers' Shangri-La.'

The back seat returned to silence and darkness. At the best of times Rogers tended to look on the darker side of life, and the wretchedness of Lagos pressed down like a suffocating blanket. His own son was three and - it seemed to him - loved his father without reservation. He'd been taken to a Midlands airport the previous month to meet Rogers returning from an overseas trip. The sight of his father on the tarmac had been unexpected and the boy had run forward whirling his arms and shrieking with delight, an image to last for ever. And perhaps it would need to last for ever, Rogers thought grimly. For the first time he looked down the years and saw how it would be in future. However he managed as a father, the balance between them was bound to shift. When the teenage years came along it would be Rogers who thought constantly about his son and came to expect little in return. The best he could hope for would be this kind of sober, managed relationship; occasional contacts through his declining years; some grief on his death, though not too much, hopefully.

His death! For God's sake, Rogers thought - that was Lagos talking. The place would dampen anyone's spirits. How did Bates stand it month after month? He made himself snap out of the mood, sit up straighter in the back of the car. He tried to think of something cheerful, like staring down on the night lights of Lagos as the Boeing left them behind.

Bates parked the car and gave his 'idiot's introduction' to the terminal, and then Rogers left him there to say the awkward goodbyes. When he looked back Bates had a hand on his son's elbow. No doubt a farewell hug would be acceptable in the circumstances.

He started on the series of encounters with airport officials that with luck would get him to the departure lounge. Check-in, immigration, security, were all negotiated, then another control point that served no apparent purpose beyond an opportunity for graft. At each stop came the demands, made without much preamble: 'something for me', 'you have naira', 'give me money now'. Rogers had some Nigerian currency left, and doled the stuff out. It was a debasing business but the thought of some wrong move provoking a delay, leading at worst to more time spent in Lagos, was insupportable.

He made it through to the departure lounge and parked himself disconsolately on a plastic seat. Other passengers arrived in dribs and drabs. The bearded irrigation engineer stomped in and sat opposite. They nodded at each other.

'What a place,' Rogers whinged. 'These constant demands for money.'

'I didn't give them a thing,' said the bearded guy.

~ Behind the curtains ~

In retirement Rogers soon learnt to pick out other men on the estate who were free from the pressure of work. The indicators were there if you cared to look for them: the men's leisurely movements; the over-walking of the dog; the small but steady decline into scruffy dress, or sprouting of facial stubble. His sense of fellowship with these individuals could change to irritation if one of them flaunted the lineaments of his condition, like the bloke of Rogers's age who plodded along with a little haversack on his back and only conversed about ailments. But then irritation was also sparked by any signs of self-righteous busyness amongst the employed; the little chap down the road, for instance, whose lawn-mowing and car-cleaning were executed with such unvarying Methodist briskness.

It was customary in the village to say hello to strangers passed on the pavements, but few encounters developed into anything that could be called conversation. However with Ken Bagley the existence of a mutual acquaintance (albeit a very slight one on Rogers's side) meant that they started to swap a few words when meeting on the High Street, or the road they both lived in. Bagley was easy to spot, in winter anyway, with his Russian-style fur hat and slow, deliberate manner of walking. He was grave but friendly.

'Oh, I'm OK,' Bagley had said once, after the ritual exchange of 'how-are-you's'.

It had sounded no more vulnerable than 'not so bad' or 'can't complain' (the sort of grudging rejoinders used by the over-60s) but something in Bagley's tone made Rogers ask again.

'Are you all right?'

'Oh, you know…'

'I don't know. What's it about, Ken?'

'Oh, don't start me on that. It's not always easy. You won't know it, but my wife suffers from depression. Has done for years. She doesn't go out. Doesn't like me going out for that matter. I'll have to hurry back now or she starts to fret.'

'Is she on medication?'

'God yes. Has been for years. Trouble is it turns her into a zombie.'

'What does she do all day?'

'Not much. I get her books from the library but she can't concentrate for long. Puts the TV on sometimes. Or stares at the blank screen.'

Rogers knew, at least, that depression was an illness, not just someone feeling a bit pissed off with life. You couldn't say 'pull yourself together', however much you wanted to. Beyond that he'd no direct experience of the condition. He realised though that things couldn't be easy for the person cast willy nilly in the role of carer. Now that he took the trouble to look he could see Bagley's skin had a pallid, desiccated appearance, almost other-worldly. Yes, that was it, the man was like a ghost. That way he had of moving, very deliberately, as if without using muscles.

'It can't be easy for you,' he said inadequately.

'I get by. I have to.' Bagley was looking embarrassed. 'Look, sorry to bother you with this. I don't tell people normally.'

'You didn't bother me - I asked.' Rogers pointed down the High Street. 'Shall we walk back together?'

'I've got to visit the Post Office.' Making an effort to lighten the mood, Bagley pointed to Rogers's corduroy cap, which had been with him for many years. 'Anyway, I'm not sure I want to be seen out with that hat of yours.'

Rogers grinned, said goodbye, and walked back alone through the modern estate they both inhabited. In the spring sunshine broad lawns at the front of detached houses gave the place an agreeable rural appearance. Most of the residents took trouble with flowers too, so that a stroll down Rogers's road was like an informal garden open day. One blot was the number of cars parked on forecourts - at least two per house, typically - but then Rogers was unusual in disliking cars; most residents would have found nothing to object to. This was a pleasant, regular, above all safe (Neighbourhood Watch) area to live in. In fact it was rare for anything to happen in his road that would have been worthy of comment at all. Occasionally someone spied a pair of foxes sitting placidly on the little green half way down. That was as outrageous as it got.

Rogers wasn't heartless - at least, he liked to think not - but within half an hour of their meeting he'd forgotten about Ken Bagley's problems. He might never have considered them again had there not been a ring at his doorbell one weekday morning, when he was alone in the house. He opened the door to find Bagley standing outside, minus hat, minus coat - just slacks and cardigan.

'Hel-lo!' he cried, temporising during the search for Bagley's Christian name, which had been mislaid in his failing memory. He was surprised. Notwithstanding the meeting and greeting on pavements neighbours rarely knocked at each other's doors, still less crossed thresholds. 'Hello, Ken' (the name suddenly returning).

Even through his brief moment of disorientation Rogers was aware of something being wrong. There was a wild look in his visitor's eyes, out of keeping with the sedate surroundings.

'I'm so sorry,' Bagley said, in a voice that was almost a howl. 'I am sorry. How could I have been so rude.'

'What?' Rogers was completely perplexed now. 'What d'you mean? What are you supposed to have done?'

'About your hat. What I said. How I could've...I don't know...'

Bagley was almost incoherent. There were thoughts in his head, obviously, but the words seemed to be coming out in the wrong order. Hat? Something about a hat? Vaguely Rogers recalled a jocular remark about his headware. Could it really be that? He thought quickly. There seemed to be only two possible explanations for Bagley's appearance on the doorstep in such a state: either he really was obsessed with the hat comment, in which case he wasn't himself; or he wanted to talk about something else. 'Whatever' - as Rogers's teenage son would have said - it seemed a good idea to get him into the house.

'That hat? But it's disgusting. My wife's threatening to burn it. Look, come in, Ken.'

'Oh no, no - I can't.' Bagley was genuinely reluctant. 'My wife...'

'Bugger it. Give yourself a break. I was about to have a cup of tea. Come and join me.'

'Well, I...'

'Come on, you daft apath.'

He grasped a sleeve as Bagley crossed the door-step looking wildly around, like a man being lured against his will to all manner of depraved pleasures. In the lounge Bagley subsided onto the sofa, his last reserves of energy apparently squandered in entering the house. Rogers left him there and went to put the kettle on.

'What is it, Ken?' he said on the way back. 'You look completely, utterly bloody pissed off with life.'

'I'm sorry...'

'Don't apologise, please. Is it your wife's illness?'

'You can't imagine. It gets on top of me sometimes.'

'Christ, I bet it does. In effect, you're a 24-hour a day carer. No nurse would undertake the job, not even for a fortune.'

'You take your marriage vows, don't you.'

'Not like that, you don't. It must be a total nightmare. I tell you, Ken, I think you're a hero. I mean it.' He did, too.

Bagley raised a limp hand. 'Don't be nice to me please. I can't answer for what might happen.'

Rogers brought them mugs of tea. It was quite outside his usual routine, two old blokes sitting around drinking tea in the middle of the morning. I'll be going to tupperware parties next, he thought, or an Ann Summers evening. Bagley had a few sips and left the rest to get cold. He seemed less desperate now, but lifeless.

'It's always the little things in marriage,' he said. 'Do you find that?'

'Tell me about it.' Some small action, a tiny remark, that revived the a lifelong battlefield underlying it; the elegant surface of the iceberg, the vast, gloomy expanse concealed beneath.

'I do a bit of writing,' Bagley said surprisingly. 'Poetry, mostly. It keeps me going, to tell the truth. Why am I telling you this? Well, for that sort of thing, you have to get away by yourself and concentrate. Nothing worthwhile comes while you're sitting in front of the television. My wife, poor thing, she doesn't like me to be absent, even in another room. I'm supposed to sit there with her - saying nothing, doing nothing. So I can't get to grips with the one thing that...'

Rogers waited for him to finish the sentence ('...that keeps me sane?'), but when it didn't happen, he said 'She can't help herself, I suppose.'

It was a foolish remark since Bagley was racked with guilt already; he knew better than anyone that his wife 'couldn't help it'. 'I know, I know,' he said. 'But I can't stop myself resenting these things. All I have to do for her, and she won't...it goes round and round in my head. I'm a poor thing, aren't I?'

'You're bloody not.'   Change the record, Rogers thought, and asked 'Tell me more about your writing.' He tried a bit of writing himself, but hadn't seen Bagley as a literary type, or an intellectual at all. The bloke dressed conservatively, had that odd, gliding walk, the etiolated features and veiled expression. As far as he knew Bagley's work before retirement had been in a printing firm.

'Oh, it's personal stuff. The usual sort of thing. It gives me pleasure, anyway.'

'Ever thought about getting it published?'

'There's a little writing co-operative in town I go to. They put my stuff in from time to time. I can drop a copy round if you'd like to see it.'

'I'd love to see it.' Rogers tried to fit his expression to the words. Reading amateur verse was worse than tooth extraction, especially if comment was called for; he found it hard to lie with conviction about that sort of thing.

Bagley's literary efforts came through the letter box a couple of days later, when Rogers had (again) all but forgotten the conversation. There were two poems, amongst a dozen other contributions from would-be writers, all word-processed onto A4 sheets stapled between lurid orange paper covers. Most of the stuff was pretty ordinary, but not Bagley's. One of the poems presented a personal philosophy, a sensitive statement of life's subtle virtues intercut with natural images, a piece worthy of a place in any published anthology. Rogers read it half a dozen times.

After that he started to give Bagley more thought. If he felt admiration of the poem it was mixed with envy, not to mention irritation that he could recognise the work's quality but not come even near to emulating it - a sort of Salieri/Mozart syndrome. The incongruity!: such angelic language, deeply-felt sentiments, emerging from Bagley's crumbling figure, the stolid frame in mackintosh and fur hat wandering down to shop at Somerfields. Rogers tried to visualise strangers watching himself on the same errand. What would they think him capable of from the mere evidence of a figure in an overcoat? Some comparable artistic achievement? Or more everyday accomplishments: understanding and kindness to friends and neighbours; sensitive love-making, even, if not now, at least in the past.

Doubtless few of their neighbours knew what Bagley had to endure when he ambled through the front door of his detached house: the daily struggles between the unwitting monster his wife had become and that other gentle monster - as Bagley saw it, himself. No-one knew that a handful of poems word-processed for an informal publication were keeping Bagley sane, holding the nightmare at bay. The formal indicators of community gave little away: comings and goings, cheerful greetings on pavements, the drawn curtains, parked cars, glimpses into mattress-filled garages, angry buzz of lawnmowers, wheelie-bins.

~ Nor the years condemn ~

A faint groan of traffic drifted from the Cambridge Road across the gravestones in Edmonton cemetery. Rogers had been hoping for a grey and drizzly day - the kind he liked best - but the sun shone brightly. He stood beside his father's grave hand in hand with his 5-year old son Luke. Twenty years had gone by since he'd last seen the stone. It had taken some finding after such an interval. Eventually he'd recognised the shape of the rectangular plot containing the graves of two dozen RAF men. The dedication simply gave his father's name and a brief quotation.

Luke pointed to the inscribed words. 'What does that say?'

'It says "We shall remember them".'

Luke leant forward to examine the inscription, though he couldn't begin to read it. 'Was your daddy on the red side?'

Rogers laughed. In a hazy grasp of recent history, his son seemed to be confusing the North Atlantic Alliance with Manchester United.

'It wasn't like that,' he told him.

'Do you?' Luke asked.

'Do I what?'

'Do you remember them?'

'That's an interesting question, Luke.'

Luke had been the one who'd asked to see this grave, but his attention was already on something else. He'd got hold of a stick and was turning over half a dead worm that lay in the grass. The subject of worms was one Rogers didn't care to dwell upon, on his own account or Luke's. It was hard, tackling death with a 5-year old. He wanted to explain that the person represented by this grave would have been Luke's 'other' grandfather but it was all too complicated, and potentially upsetting. How did his son feel at this moment? Violent death seemed the last thing on his mind as he bent over the stick chuntering away. Yet something of this visit would find its way into the boy's subconscious; all the books said so. Rogers had been the same age when the RAF telegram came, and he still had a memory of his mother's house filling up with relatives. Apparently his comment (well, he was only five) had been 'We won't be getting a car now, will we?' He couldn't remember the telegram's actual arrival; nor any personal sense of loss at the time.

He tried to home in on his own feelings now as Luke pottered beside him. A yard from where they stood, under the earth, were the bones of the man who'd given him an existence. But he'd never known his father, and recalling the Liberator's crash brought no misty-eyed emotion. What, then? A misfortune. An always missing something. A sombre edge to his mood on this sunny afternoon. That was all. It was a tragedy for his mother all right, though she'd never have used the word.

'Let's go?' This was Luke, who reckoned he'd exhausted the cemetery's possibilities.

Rogers drove down to Lower Edmonton Green, past All Saints church where he'd been a choirboy. The buildings whizzed by, curiously unfamiliar considering he'd have passed them several times a week in his teens. Then he realised why. In those days nobody had cars; the route had to be walked. On Sundays (morning and evensong), he must have spent an hour and a half on the hoof.

He continued on to Upper Edmonton, down Brettenham Road where he'd gone to primary school, and parked in the road where his mother had lived for fifty years. Early on, the working class families used to live near each other; his mother's brother, sister, mother and mother-in-law all less than a ten-minute walk away. Now an influx of West Indian immigrants had transformed the area. Yet by chance his mother's terrace of eight houses had stayed the same, the residents growing old together, living as they'd always lived, stopping for a word on each other's doorsteps but never going in, getting sick, dying.

He held his son at shoulder height so he could use the knocker. Rogers knew the exact quality of knock needed on that door but Luke gave it a tremendous crash.

'Lord, boy, you'll wake the dead,' said his mother as she let them into the hallway. 'Come on in.'

'Can you wake the dead, Grandma?' Luke asked.

She gave Rogers a look over her glasses. 'I've started something now, haven't I?'.

'We've just come from the cemetery,' Rogers reminded her.

'I've not been down there for years,' she said. 'No, Luke, you can't. It's just a way of speaking.' Immensely sensible with children, as always, she spoke with greater vigour than usual, as if some of Luke's energy has passed into her failing frame. But then she always put on a show of robustness when someone called. Typically, she had nothing to ask about her husband's grave. 'I'll make some tea,' she called, already by the kitchen stove. What do you like to drink, Luke?'

'Do you have orange juice?'

'I do. I'll bring some.'

Rogers eased himself into the visitor's chair. Sounds of his mother making tea in the kitchen were familiar and reassuring. Coming back to this house was like re-entering the womb; and almost as constricting, given the lack of space. The place was in his bones, every inch of it. Because they'd come straight from the cemetery, he sought out signs of his father, still to be detected some forty years after that abrupt disappearance: on the sideboard, a silver cigarette case (though no-one smoked any more) decorated with the RAF wings; on the window-sill the framed photograph of him, unfathomable in RAF uniform and cap. Upstairs on the dresser, Rogers knew, would be the jewelled wrist-watch his father had brought back from America, arriving unexpectedly to a family knees-up at his parents' house and thrusting it at his wife in the hallway ('Hold on to this. It's for you'). Dangerous, exciting days.

'What was that?' said Luke.

Rogers knew the sound: the postman bringing mail, its falling from letter-box to the door-mat below. 'Will you bring it, Luke?'

'A letter,' he told his mother as she came from the kitchen with a tray.

'A big one,' she said, taking a thick A4 envelope from Luke's hands. 'What could it be, Luke?'

'Is it to do with dinosaurs?' (Luke's current preoccupation).

Rogers guessed that his mother's usual post consisted, if anything, of bills, requests from charities, other bumf. The last regular correspondent, her sister-in-law Nellie, had died three months earlier at the age of 88.

When she tore open the envelope, dozens of letters fell out.

'Good Lord,' she said, and after a moment's investigation. 'It's from Gay. She's returned all my letters to Nellie. All those she could find, anyway. Goodness knows what we'll find here.' She poked around a bit more. 'They're in date order too. Nellie was always very organised. This lot must go back to the war.' She plucked one at random from the top of the pile and peered at it. 'Well I never.'

'What?' Rogers asked.

'Listen to this. It's from when your father got his whatsit.'

'His whatsit?'

'Oh you know - his DFC.'

'Ah. Can you see to read it all right?'

'Just about. My eyes are bad, I know, but I'm OK in short bursts. Listen. It's dated July 1943. "Dear Nellie. I'm not supposed to tell you this, but I've got to tell someone or bust. I've just heard from John and it seems there's some amazing news...".' The letter went on to describe - supposedly in veiled terms, though the censors would certainly not have approved - the action that led to his father's medal. He'd sunk a U-boat, got away from some German fighters, and landed the Liberator on one wheel. '"Well, what do you think of that,"' the letter had ended up after a colourful account. '"I can't even begin to describe how I feel, Nellie. It worries me, of course, John getting into all this danger, but I'm so excited and proud too. I'm all over the place today. Will tell you more once I hear about it myself..."'

As she read, the years fell away. Her voice sounded higher and younger. Rogers could imagine his mother as she'd been forty years before. She was excited all over again, re-living the moment. Even Luke looked excited, though he didn't know why. As the letter ended she brushed away a tear. Rogers couldn't remember the last time he'd seen her cry. She was relentlessly unsentimental, like many women of her generation. 'We were very good,' she'd said once, about Nellie and herself at the funeral. 'We didn't cry.' At some point all his father's letters to her had gone on the fire, a symbolic act. 'Stop moping,' she'd have told herself. 'Concentrate on bringing up his children.' Rogers had often regretted their loss.

'Don't cry, Grandma,' said Luke, in the matter-of-fact way she'd so often used herself.

'Well, well,' said Rogers, pouring some tea and handing over the cup.

'I know.' She was already herself again. 'If you'll get me the brown album at the bottom of the bookcase, I'll show you that plane after it landed.'

Luke jumped up. 'I'll get it.'

It was the usual RAF photo, the plane (much the worse for wear) with a bunch of grinning idiots standing in front of it, most of them marked down to die. Not for the first time Rogers wished he could get behind the heroism, know what his father had really been like. No-one gave a war hero's sons information, but for the hoary old routines. ('Your father was a fine man, blah, blah'.) 'Age shall not weary them, nor the years condemn'; the poem's sentiments were double-edged, or ought to have been. He grabbed a quick look at his mother. The skin hung in folds from her face. She looked so old when Luke was about.

Rogers got up and climbed the stairs to the toilet. It was one of the few innovations in the house, supplanting the 'outside loo' in the garden, where they used to have old copies of the Daily mirror for paper. Going down again, he could hear Luke prattling away and his mother's easy responses. He sat on the stairs for a moment, to give them time on their own. The pattern of light passing through glass panes in the door was infinitely familiar. Into his head came an imagined image of 'that telegram' falling through the letter-box (the same one) onto the mat; his mother coming into the hall, seeing it, guessing what it meant. Where would she have stopped to read the wretched thing? It was something that had never occurred to him before. In those days he and his brother would have been romping about in the dining room. She probably sat where he was now, seeing the words, not wanting to; knowing that the hard years stretched ahead. Then came the business of contacting relatives - no telephones, of course - and the full household that was perhaps his first memory.

When he re-entered the lounge she was still looking at the airmen in the photo. Luke had lots of questions, and she'd been answering with the easy frankness that happened between grandma and grandson, not always replicated with closer generations. He was asking about the stocky-looking young man on the end of the row. She half-stopped her answer when Rogers came in, then plunged ahead.

'His name was Peter Bunn. He was the flight engineer.'

'What's "engineer"?'

'He's the man who looks after the engine of the plane. He has lots of spanners and screwdrivers, that sort of thing.'

'Daddy's no good with a spanner.'

'Hah! You're telling me, Luke.'

An instinct told Rogers to stay out of their way, and he went to sit on the sofa at the other end of the room, almost forgotten by mother and son.

'Did you know Peter Bunn?' Luke asked.

'Oh yes, I met him many times. I used to go out with all of them when

I stayed with my husband at the airfield.'

'Was he a nice man, Peter Bunn?'

'He was a very nice man, Luke.'

'Where is he now?'

'I wish I knew.' She was almost talking to herself, as Luke's questions unwittingly pushing the right buttons. 'He came to see me sometimes after the war, but he wasn't himself. He said he had to get away. I can't remember where. He did tell me.'

Rogers actually remembered a strange man visiting when he was small. His mother and the man had sat in this same room, one each side of the coal fire, talking closely. It was unusual, and even at this distance he remembered his feeling of exclusion.

'He used to live in Brodie Road,' she went on in quiet reverie. 'Whenever I got the bus to Manor House I passed the end of his road. I always thought of him.'

The sky outside the window was heavy with storm clouds. The house had always been quiet, and the room now was dark and silent as a tomb. Rogers sat still, fascinated, feeling excluded all over again. He wasn't ready for these revelations. He was used to his mother in a clearly labelled box: 'war widow, courageously brought up sons on her own, now old and semi-dependent on them, devoted to memory of dead husband'. It had taken Luke's innocent questions to ruffle the image. 'Nor the years condemn.' But the living weren't fossilised like the dead; they had their moments, even in old age; their uncertainties, misdemeanours. He could relate to that himself.

Luke jumped to his feet, piping up in a shrill voice. 'Oh look! There's a cat in the garden.'

~ Keeping a ghost happy ~

Cocoa the cat crossed the kitchen floor and rubbed herself against Rogers's trouser leg. Since the demise of her mistress - of which she was presumably unaware - the cat had become a bit more sociable, especially towards Rogers, who fed her. He bent to empty some of the noxious cat meat into the dish and added some Whiskas biscuits. Not noticeably off her food, Cocoa immediately lowered her head to these offerings. How had she been affected, Rogers wondered. Of course the abrupt disappearance of the person she'd lived with for the past four years would be disorienting, or puzzling, or deeply upsetting - whatever passed for these emotions in the feline world. On the other hand Cocoa did not actually know that she would never see her companion again, would never hear her voice. Rogers couldn't help feeling the animal had the best of it.

   He wondered whether cats noticed things like the state of the kitchen floor, cleaner than it had ever been, in preparation for visits by aspiring tenants, or the piecemeal disappearance of furniture to the point where rooms were stripped down to carpets and skirting boards. Cocoa would - he supposed - be aware that larger items had gone; tables, chairs, beds, the stuff that imposed upon her low-slung world. She would surely not have missed the dozens of ornaments, like the cut-glass flower vase that had stood in his mother's sight for the past 60 years; nor for that matter her old copy of The grapes of wrath, which Rogers had read when 16 and which his own son was now reading at home.

He looked at his watch: 10.30, the time arranged for the visit of a Mrs Brampton and her daughter. Now the moment had come to throw the place open, he wanted to keep it to himself for a little longer. He'd often come here alone in the weeks since his mother's death. He could still feel her presence in the house; in the kitchen where she sat before lunch doing the Daily mail crossword, in the lounge where she lay in her mechanical chair watching TV. He walked through the rooms for the umpteenth time, then threw open the kitchen door to look at the garden, the only part of the property that had stayed as it used to be. In hospital his mother had asked him to describe the flowers in bloom; her son, whom she well knew could identify three flowers from the whole panoply in the kingdom.

The bell rang and he opened the front door to a stout middle-aged woman and a teenage girl with green hair. He'd expected a sense of desecration as the first visitors clumped down the hallway but it wasn't like that. He toured them through the bungalow's five rooms, then left the pair to go round on their own. They were back in five minutes saying they liked the house and wanted to live there.

Cocoa had fled when they walked into the kitchen but Mrs Brampton spotted a tail disappearing through the cat-flap.

'You've a cat,' she said.

'My mother had. My brother will be giving it a home soon.'

'We'll be bringing two with us.'

He'd already begun to dislike her. Certain forms of conduct were suitable for prospective tenants - diffidence, cautious explorations, conditional tenses - and Mrs Brampton seemed to be unaware of them.

Still, he tried not to rule the woman out straight away. 'There's a cat home in the village,' he said in an attempt at helpfulness, 'For when people go on holiday.'

'Oh, I would certainly not put my cat in such a place.' Mrs Brampton said. 'Most definitely not. My cats are not accustomed to sharing their lives with other cats.' She frowned at the Whiskas packet and intoned as if reading from a sacred book. 'My cats never eat cat food. My cats are fed on chicken and turkey slices, with chocolates for afters.'

'You mean they're spoilt,' Rogers observed.

'Yes.' The daughter spoke up cheerfully.

The daughter, intelligent and straightforward, was called Tracey. He tried to talk to her about school and GCSE's but Mrs Brampton wanted to dominate the conversation. Tracey didn't seem to mind. She clearly thought her mother was a bit of a card. Rogers thought how it was that families got accustomed to the peculiarities of their members, while outsiders found them strange. He used to be taken aback by a friend who lay down on his parents' kitchen floor after a meal. No doubt the Bramptons, mother and daughter, would have been surprised by the lack of overt affection between Rogers and his mother; how he'd only told her 'I love you' when the body lay shedding its warmth in the hospital bed.

Mrs Brampton was talking. He was aware that he'd missed some of her remarks, but it didn't seem to matter. She was happier holding forth than entering into a dialogue. The talk was an irksome mixture of assertiveness and diffidence. 'I'm afraid we're staunch Catholics,' she said at one point. Why 'afraid', he wondered. Some of the most fucked-up people he'd ever known had been Catholics but you didn't let a house on the basis of religious beliefs. 'We're not narrow people,' was another of her observations, made at least twice. She had a knack of putting such unexceptional views in an aggravating way.

By now his only thought was to get the woman out. He made a couple of 'moving towards the door' motions which she just stood and watched, before telling her (inaccurately) that he had another appointment. He invented two more sets of people coming to look at the bungalow and said he'd let her know by the end of the week.

He closed the front door behind the Bramptons and stood in the hallway relishing the silence as it surged back into the bungalow. He could hear his mother's voice very clearly, that unmistakable quirky texture, unassuming but sure. 'For heaven's sake, Michael,' she was saying, 'Don't let the place to that dreadful woman.' His mother had two epithets to describe people who'd merited her disapproval: 'funny packet' for the milder cases, and 'dodgy baggage' for the occasional one who fell into her blackest books. He'd no doubt that Mrs Brampton would have been a dodgy baggage.

Cocoa had come back through the cat flap and was just inside the kitchen door staring up at him. The two of them stood like statues in a museum. Perhaps the cat had been staring there when his mother fell, on the spot where Rogers now stood, where he'd come round and found her when there was no answer to his phone calls. There would have been the same quality of silence outside, in this quietest of roads; and inside, too, except - as now - for the familiar burbling of the central heating system.

Rogers had no religious beliefs to fall back on: nothing unhealthily complex (I'm afraid we're staunch Catholics) and not even a simple, permissive creed like the views of a Buddhist friend. He knew with unflinching certainty that his mother's ashes were the only residue of her long life, and that they'd been scattered on his father's grave at Edmonton cemetery. For some reason he'd never felt the same certainty about ghosts. Where the notion of speaking to God merely led to a fit of the giggles, he was readily open to the prospect of a phantasm. It sounded absurd but he half expected his mother to make an appearance. She was in his dreams almost daily; why not here too, where she had spent the last five years of her life? Surely she would come limping in from the darkness of the hallway. He would see her and not be afraid.

The one item of furniture that remained in the house was her mechanical chair, a great upholstered affair that dominated the lounge and contorted itself this way and that in response to an operating wand. His mother had spent hours in its padded embrace. Rogers had the sudden conviction that she was there now, lying on the extravagant cushions. The sense of her in the bungalow was so powerful. Cocoa too was staring expectantly at the lounge door. She was there all right. Rogers even said something on his way in, something like 'All right, I'm coming.

His sudden movement sent the neurotic Cocoa skittering away again, and when he reached the room the chair stood empty. Not finding her there was almost as much of a shock as finding her would have been. He spoke anyway.

'Don't worry, Mum - I'll not let the place to that woman. She'd drive you clean up the wall, wouldn't she?'

He'd known they would see eye to eye on the subject.

~ Anorak country ~

Setting off to London for the Randy Newman concert, Rogers noticed a middle-aged man with a movie camera at the village railway station. There was no-one else around. The bloke was on the platform opposite, standing there intently, camera extended, filming the empty track and the signal on red. A signal! Rogers wondered who would bother to film a railway signal, but that's what was happening all right. The word 'anorak' sprang irresistibly to mind. The guy even wore an anorak. He was still filming as the train came in and pulled away again with Rogers on it.

Three hours later Rogers joined up with Stuart outside the Festival Hall box office. They'd known each other a few months after meeting at a cricket match and been to a couple of gigs since then. A friendship in the making. Rogers hoped so, anyway. Stuart was the most civilised and quirky of companions. They shared this enthusiasm for - how would he put this? - singers (singer-songwriters, really) who were too good to make the charts. Stuart had suggested the Randy Newman concert and Rogers readily agreed. They'd travelled down separately from the Midlands.

The pair of them stood at the bar nursing their glasses, watching the audience mill about the foyer. Something was in the air, a sense of occasion. Newman rarely toured. He was offering just the single concert now. Stuart, who had a knack of spotting celebrities, nudged Rogers's arm and nodded towards a man wearing a broad-brimmed hat, angular spectacles, and an overcoat that almost touched the ground.

'Elvis Costello,' he murmured.

The big boys were turning out.

They found their seats in the auditorium. As expected, a piano was in place on the platform - Newman always accompanied himself - but there were also dozens of music stands.

'An orchestra!' Stuart exclaimed.

Events like this one lacked the predictability of a classical concert. A popular singer might be preceded by a warm-up artist, or not; might be in good voice or not. ('I really don't know how it will go tonight,' Shawn Colvin had said when they heard her in Sheffield.) A singer might go on for several hours, or for barely forty minutes; might turn up late, or drunk, or not turn up at all. You never knew. It was part of the experience.

Newman came onto the platform promptly. No warm-up. He was an interesting talker - intelligent, witty, cynical - as the songs suggested he would be. Some comment between numbers was always to be welcomed, the more revealing the better. (With Dylan you got nothing; barely an introduction to members of the band.) Newman was self-deprecating; a shock of grey hair on his head, he referred to 'looking in the bathroom mirror and spotting a touch of grey at the temples'. That got a laugh. He was resigned. 'If I die tomorrow,' he sighed, 'The obituaries will say "Randy Newman - writer of the song 'Short people'".' He gave a rendering of his nemesis, still the scourge of political correctness ('They wear platform shoes / On their nasty little feet / Well, I don't want no short people...').

The singer was in the UK to launch his new album, the first for many years. He gave them the songs from it, one after the other. The peculiar quality of this artist began to take hold. You could never say that Randy Newman was 'in good voice', for he scarcely had a voice at all. (That had been unimportant since the invention of the microphone.) His crafty inflexions and intonations carried the listener along. And the words, like no other lyricist's! Some of his stuff read like a crazy passage from The economist. 'The great nations of Europe' was followed by 'The world isn't fair' ('When Karl Marx was a boy...'). The personal stuff, when it came - like 'I'm dead (but I don't know it)' - was shocking by contrast, though he hammed up the rendering of that one to shield his audience from any disquietude.

Before the interval he did one called 'I miss you' - 'written for my first wife'. The dedication had echoes of Thomas Hardy, who wrote reams of love poetry on the death of his ex. In both cases you wondered what the second wife thought. You especially wondered when the song was performed; when you heard the passion and regret, the reiterated line ('I miss you / I miss you / I miss you / I miss you...') with a repeated drum beat behind it. Rogers found himself in familiar, captivating territory: the first hearing of a special song, not as yet fully grasped; the invasion of his senses; the knowledge that he would return to it over and over again. All that pleasure in store. You got one of those every other album, if you were very lucky. In the middle of it Newman forgot the lyrics; recovered himself. He went into the interval upset, throwing out a line about memory and senility. To Rogers the lapse didn't matter a jot. If anything it gave the song something extra. He felt like a philatelist who'd bought a stamp with a misprint, its value increased.

They took their interval drinks onto the balcony and stood leaning over it, watching the Thames go past.

'What's this new album called?' Rogers asked.

'Bad something or other,' said Stuart.

'Bad love.' The voice came from a robust-looking chap, fiftyish, alone, also holding a drink.

'Is it good?' Rogers included them both in the question.

'It's wonderful.' The bloke spoke quietly, almost in veneration.'

The three of them started talking about music. Nothing personal; quite possibly the guy thought Rogers and Stuart were a gay couple. This man - they never got his name - knew a lot. He went to gigs 'whenever he could', he told them. You saw many such enthusiasts, trailing their favourites all around the UK. Rogers was one of them himself.

'Give me a name,' he urged the bloke. 'Someone new, someone I really should try out.'

'Good grief! What a proposition! All right then. Out of the blue, Sarah McLachlan.'

Rogers took out a pen and wrote the name down.

The newcomer mentioned another name. 'That one's got a blues tinge about him,' he said.

'There was an episode of The Simpsons the other day,' Stuart told them. 'The daughter was listening to an old blues trombonist in a city underpass - don't ask me why. Then she got out her clarinet and played a blues solo herself. "That's good blues," said the old musician. "Yeah, but I still don't feel any better," said the girl. "The blues ain't to make you feel better," said the old musician. "It's to make other people feel worse".

They all liked the story.

'You have to be careful recommending singers,' the bloke went on. 'I've got a business acquaintance I play golf with. He knows I go to gigs - people he's never heard of. He doesn't understand why I bother, because he's...well, he's just out of that stuff. He makes money, that's his thing. Still, he asked me once what sort of music I liked. Couple of weeks later my phone rang and this guy was on the other end, ranting and raving. "Listen," he was yelling down the line, "Listen to this...horse manure. I paid money for this." It was Tom Waits, doing that groaning stuff of his, you know what I mean. Admittedly an acquired taste. "You recommended this," the guy was going on. "Are you insane, or what?" The man stopped to summarise: 'That's why I'm a bit cautious when it comes to recommendations.'

'I won't hold you to account over this Sarah woman,' Rogers told him. 'But finding new stuff is a problem. How do you manage?'

'Just keep my ears open, I suppose. The radio. Never miss the Bob Harris show.'

'Bob Harris?' Rogers didn't know the name, and Stuart also shook his head.

'Radio 2, Saturdays, late evening,' the man told them.

'Oh I see,' said Rogers. 'But that'll clash with Match of the day.'

'You need earphones,' the bloke said. 'I have Match of the day with the sound turned down, Bob on the earphones. My wife thinks it's anti-social, but what can you do?'

The show finished and the three men went their separate ways. That Saturday Rogers listened to the Bob Harris show (though not until Match of the day had finished). Harris played pop/rock numbers from every point on the spectrum. He talked a good deal between tracks, except when playing an appealing number by a woman singer. After that one he simply said 'Sarah McLachlan'. He said it in a special, tender sort of way.

Rogers went out and bought the Bad love album. He played 'I miss you' again and again until he wife complained. He also bought a Sarah McLachlan CD and for a short while became obsessed with her. A new singer! It was like a friendship developing: the past, to be slowly uncovered; the unknown future to be anticipated. (Rogers's enthusiasm was shared - a rare circumstance, this - by his 18-year old son, who for unexplained reasons always referred to the singer as 'Sarah McChicken'.)

Rogers also looked up Harris's web site on the Internet. On the interactive section he sent the DJ a note. He mentioned their interval companion at the Newman concert. He described the man's habit of listening to The Bob Harris show through earphones while watching Match of the day. Harris sent a brief reply. Later Rogers wished he'd requested a McLachlan track for the guy. He felt they were all linked through the freemasonry of enthusiasm, for Newman, for McLachlan, for that whole scene.

The bloke's golfing companion - the one who railed against Tom Waits - he was out of the loop.

Returning from the Newman concert that day, Rogers had stepped off the train at his village station and remembered the morning scene; the anorak religiously filming the railway signal. Everyone needs a passion, he thought. If you could choose one - rather than (which was what actually happened) have the passion choose you - he'd settle for something that could inspire the note of tender reverence: 'Sarah McLachlan' - two reverent words coming over the ether, dropped into the silence between tracks. A passion pretty much identical to what he'd got, in fact. But anything would be better than nothing; anything at all. It might mean lying on a cold garage floor assembling bits of motorbike (the very last passion for Rogers himself). Or breeding ferrets in the back yard. Or standing at a village station filming a railway signal on red.

~ Dog and bone ~

Rogers called at the centre half an hour before his talk to collect a package of pens and leaflets from the pigeon holes. He operated the security code in the front door, was let in from above, and climbed the stairs to the operations room. Lights were on in the late afternoon gloom and the curtains were partially drawn. Two women sat there in the familiar, homely surroundings. Christine, in her late fifties, was on the phone. She wore a woollen twin-set with a string of pearls at the neck. Frieda was in a flowery dress. She was seated by her phone reading a book and eating something involving chocolate. She made a little gesture of greeting. He knew precisely how old Frieda was, as she'd celebrated her 84th birthday during their last duty together.

'I'm afraid I shall have to terminate this call,' Christine was saying, her cut-glass accent blithely unperturbed. She put the receiver down and sat back with a sigh. 'Another wanker,' she said. 'What a sad little berk!'

'We get more of them than we used to,' Frieda replied in her forthright way. 'I had three in a row last week, all coming - or so they told me. You should be careful with that word 'berk', Christine. It means "cunt".'

'Does it really, Frieda?' Christine's tone suggested a mild interest.

'So I'm told.' Frieda enjoyed using taboo words. One of her favourite sayings was 'Pricks have caused much of the trouble in this world'. She also enjoyed working at Samaritans, where she could say almost anything. The trouble was, she couldn't shock the volunteers; they were waterproof. She swung her swivel chair round towards Rogers. 'And what are you doing here, pray?'

'I've come in for some materials. I'm giving a talk half an hour from now.'

'Where's it at?'

'Some sheltered flats. Er...' He consulted his instruction sheet. 'A place called St Mary's.'

'McBride Street?'

'That's the one. I'm impressed by your local knowledge, Frieda.'

'Don't be. I once visited my aunt there.'

'I see. Perhaps I'll meet her, then.'

'No you won't.' Frieda took a savage mouthful of Waggon Wheel. 'She dropped off the hooks years ago. People go to those places to die.'

Rogers had been around long enough to disregard Frieda's bark, which was much worse than her bite. He knew that when the phone rang she would instantly become a monument of tact and sympathy. He never tired of watching such transformations; nor of hearing ladies in twinset and pearl outfits discuss 'wanking'.

He picked up his stuff from the pigeon holes and left Frieda and Christine to their duties. 'St Mary's' was down a cul de sac in a part of

Leicester he'd never visited before. He drove right past the road once, then returned and parked outside a building that looked more secure than Alcatraz. A woman answered his ring and let him inside. Her lapel badge said 'Catherine Bolton, Facilitator', but they introduced themselves anyway.

They were in a long corridor with doors on either side. Something about the paintwork, or maybe it was the carpeting, gave the place an institutional air.

'I'd appreciate a loo before we start,' Rogers told the woman.

'Oh, we've got plenty of those.'

She led him to one of the anonymous doors. Behind it was a spacious cubicle, more like a squash court than a toilet. There were steel rails and handles everywhere, for inmates to heave themselves on and off the porcelain. An alarm buzzer was set into the wall. He noticed other equipment, not immediately identifiable. Rogers was impressed, but also over-awed. The place made such an overt acknowledgement of its residents' frailties. He felt grateful that he would go before them with his little incapacities under wraps.

The venue for the talk was a large room with chairs arranged in a circle. The area was warm and uncluttered. Two elderly women had taken their places early, and he went to talk to them. Within a few minutes they'd told him their ages. Frances, the 92-year old, had been at the centre six years. 'I used to live in Hastings,' she told him, 'My best friend died. I phoned my daughter - she lives not far from here - and told her "I want to go into a home". "Are you sure mum?" she said. I'd always said I wouldn't, you see. I came down here for a week and we looked at St Mary's. I decided straight away.'

The other woman was called Claire, thin with a refined air, a former civil servant. Like Frances, she was keen to put her recent history on record. She was 85 and had had a stroke.

'You look fine though,' Rogers told her, with 75% frankness.

'I was paralysed down one side. That was five years ago.' Her tone was matter-of-fact; paralysis the natural corollary to such a misfortune. 'A lot of the feeling has come back. I was lucky it was my left side. I could still write, hold a tea-cup and so on from the beginning.'

'She does very well,' Frances said. The pair were self-reliant but touchingly supportive of each other.

'I admire your courage,' said Rogers, this time with total honesty.

'Oh, you have to get on with it,' Claire said.

Rogers had begun to wonder if he'd be speaking to an audience of two, but other residents were now drifting in. They moved slowly, with the help of assorted metal frames. After seven or eight women in succession, a man turned up. The bloke had a yellowish face with bruised marks under the eyes. He moved without artificial aids but precariously, like a toddler taking early steps.

They had eleven people eventually, all well over 80. Once everyone had settled down a helper came round with a trolley, offering tea and large slices of cake. He noticed Claire getting plenty of the cake into her thin figure. After that Catherine Bolton said a few words. She had one announcement: Marjorie, in room 38, had mislaid the timing device on her scooter, and hoped someone might know where to find it. Then she introduced Rogers. 'He's going to tell us about the work of Samaritans.'

He started tactfully, he hoped. 'Personally I always feel like dozing at this time of day,' he told them, 'So I don't mind a bit if you drop off.' There was a murmur of appreciation at this. He had a sheet of notes but talked mainly from memory, gazing round at the circle of dazed faces. After a while, and try as they might to resist it, his audience showed signs of drowsiness. It was painful to see Claire's head sway on her shoulders, to watch her eyelids droop and snap open again, as she forced herself to attend. The others were emulating her, heads waving like wild flowers in a breeze. He felt an immense admiration for their pluckiness. They'd abandoned their afternoon naps to hear some stranger rabbiting away about nothing much. It was a dogged exercise of will. After all, there was nothing to stop them sliding gently to oblivion. Nobody in this place was going to get better.

He skipped half his notes and ended the talk after 25 minutes. The wilting faces recomposed themselves and prepared to ask questions, encouraged by Catherine Bolton. It was clearly easier to stay conscious during the cut and thrust of question time.

There were some sensible enquiries from people in the circle, then one from a robust-looking woman sitting on her own.

'Do you have any special training before being allowed to answer calls?' she asked

Rogers said a bit about the training programme, pleased with her interest. A few moments later the woman asked exactly the same thing again. Nobody said anything.

Claire had put two interesting questions in her unassuming way. He guessed that the others admired her intellect, saw her as a sort of leader. She spoke up again. 'I think it must be depressing, listening to people who are ready to kill themselves. Doesn't it get you down?'

'It can do,' he began, 'Especially if...' He was going to say 'Especially if they're young,' but thought better of it. 'Especially in some circumstances. But when people have made up their mind to die, they're often quite calm...resigned might be a better word. When that happens, I find it easier to take.'

'It's hard to imagine,' Claire said.

'I had a recent call from a bloke in a prison cell,' he went on. He had to be careful about quoting detail, but didn't think that recounting this incident would do any harm. '"I've had enough," this man told me. "You'll see it in the papers tomorrow, know what I mean? When I make up my mind about something..." I'm sure he meant to kill himself that night, but he was so calm about it that I felt OK. Then there was an interruption from the prisoner in the next cell, and I heard my caller shout out "Just a mo, I'm on the blower". I told him, "I've not heard that expression for a long time - on the blower", and he laughed. He said "Nah - I usually say dog and bone." Rogers paused. He was thinking that actually this everyday exchange had been upsetting; more so than the man's earlier statement of intent. He didn't tell his audience this. He wondered why he'd told the story at all.

He wound up the talk soon afterwards, and Catherine Bolton gave a vote of thanks. She wrote Samaritans a cheque and also took a collection from the members of the audience. Back came the plate containing some coins and a couple of five pound notes. Rogers felt embarrassed, taking these offerings from people who were - he had no doubt - mostly strapped for cash.

His audience drifted away, some of them thanking him on the way out. He put the money in an envelope and said goodbye to the facilitator. Before going home he went back to the office to put his meagre takings in the safe. In the operations room both volunteers - a different pair now - were crouched over their phones talking. There was no opportunity for a chat. Rogers heard one of them murmur 'Are you afraid of dying?' He deposited the money, went down the stairs and left of the building. Outside, leaves were blowing about on the forecourt.

~ The old school ~

Sixty years had gone by since Rogers's previous visit to Mill Hill - the town or the school - and he was mildly surprised to find the same bus route in operation. He boarded the single-decker at Bowes Road tube station and stared through the window as the landscape rolled past: scrappy Whetstone, the abrupt end of suburbia at Totteridge, then green fields, horses at pasture and the other rural delights. It all looked quite appealing in the mild spring sunlight.

Fumbling in his pocket for a sherbet lemon, Rogers dislodged a pound coin which rolled across the gangway. It was returned by the man sitting opposite, a heavily built bloke with features half concealed by a bird's-nest beard.

Rogers thanked him. 'Not too many passengers on this route,' he said, nodding at the empty seats around them.

'Always like it,' the bearded fellow responded. "Aven't seen you on the bus before, 'ave I?'

'Not for 60 years or so. I'm on my way to Mill Hill village - to start with, anyway.'

'The bus don't go right there, y'know. 'Ow are you thinking of getting up to the village?'

The glance of inspection was brief, but Rogers knew what the man was thinking. 'I was hoping to walk it. I don't look that decrepit, do I?

My doctor says I need to walk every day.'

There was no smile, but a nod of acknowledgement. 'All right, mate, long as you know. You'll be going up by the public school then?'

'That's right.'

'Past the toffee noses.'

'Is that how you see them?'

It made for a slightly awkward conversation if the bloke had a thing about public schools. His clothes - the souwester-style hat, check shirt with rolled up sleeves, belt tied rather than fastened across substantial stomach - advertised class as much as any public schoolboy's blazer.

'Money talks and merit walks,' his companion pronounced suddenly, without explanation.

Rogers decided on a clean breast. 'I was a boy there myself, centuries ago.'

'You don't look the type.' The man's grunt could have been a sort of apology.

'I wasn't the type. My family was working class.'

'No offence, mate, but you don't look that either.'

'I suppose that's right too,' Rogers admitted. 'Who the hell am I, then?'

The question wasn't the kind that needed a reply. All the same, by accident or design the man had hit on a good point. Rogers didn't quite fit anywhere. He was neither fish nor fowl. Before going to Mill Hill on a scholarship he'd lived with his mother and brother in a downbeat suburb of North London. Their rented, terraced house had an outside toilet and no hot water. (Rogers kept clean by visiting the town hall slipper baths.) Via an averagely successful career he'd risen, if that was the word, into the middle classes. It had been nothing to do with public school; just a progression familiar to many working class boys (though clearly not to the old chap beyond the gangway).

Thinking of the past, Rogers nearly went beyond his stop. Just in time he spotted the place where he used to alight after the thrice-termly 'exeats' home. He threw a goodbye at the bearded bloke and climbed carefully down onto the pavement. For a moment he was disoriented by the sudden exit, then picked up his bearings. The way forward lay up a sloping path between railed gardens. He laboured to the top of this and leaned against a sturdy fence, wheezing madly, grateful for the overhead branches that shielded him from the sun. In a flower bed nearby was a stunning array of crocuses. Days like this threatened the measured equanimity he'd constructed against doctors' reports. Sod them, he thought, pushing off from the railings and going on at a decent pace.

Before long he passed the convent school, where girls had leaned from first floor windows to pour water on the school corps as its uniformed members route-marched past. Every step seemed to unlock memories of the Mill Hill years. Not a time of desperate unhappiness or anything like that. Just five years separate from the continuum of his life, buried in a discrete compartment of memory.

The old man felt all right again as he approached the frontage of the school, a tacky war memorial in neo-classical design. As he paused to deplore the architecture some very young Mill Hill boys strolled by, hands in pockets, blazers undone (privileges which in his day had, absurdly, been reserved for older boys). At the same moment an overweight village woman passed, shoving a push-chair with infant, and dragging on a cigarette. Through Rogers's memory flashed a schoolboy incident, notorious in its time, of three monitors walking past the war memorial with their arms linked (yet another daft privilege), wearing the straw boaters permitted in summer term. The apparition had been too much for a passing village lad who without warning had lashed out and knocked one of the monitors over.

'Toffee noses,' Rogers said conversationally to himself.

Beside the memorial a small arch led into the school grounds proper. Strictly speaking it was all private property, but security had never been an issue and Rogers ambled through to find himself amongst ancient buildings, not noticeably restored during the years since his previous sighting. A few boys were about but no-one challenged him. There had been, and still were, rows of notice-boards where staff and monitors posted up important announcements. As soon as he saw them another memory zoomed in. He'd been standing there before breakfast the morning after a general election, an election which had confirmed the return of a Conservative government. A charwoman had emerged from the school buildings on her way home after the morning shift. He recalled her clearly, a bent figure in old clothes with a shawl over her head. He heard the raucous, bitter cry with which she strafed the surprised young gentlemen in their smart blazers.

'Garn, yer bleedin' little Lord Fauntleroys,' she'd screeched, in a voice which reached to the far corners of the quadrangle. 'Gaaaarn! Yer bleedin' Tories are in again.'

Rogers pushed on, pondering the unpredictable behaviour of his memory. If asked, he'd have said that strife between schoolboys and locals hadn't been an issue in his day. And here he was already with a couple of flashbacks on that very theme. The images came and went beyond his control.

He crossed the quadrangle now and took the path which skirted the school's main rugby pitch and led eventually to Burton Bank, the house where he'd lived for five years. The view from here was almost a parody of pastoral delight. The way led downhill, past the tennis courts and between two more playing fields. On one of these some boys were in shirt-sleeves playing cricket, after converting into a wicket the same tree trunk that Rogers's contemporaries had used six decades earlier. A boy passed on the path giving him a quizzical stare. He must, he supposed, look somewhat the worse for wear. The walk between school and house, which he used to make three or four times a day, had been further than he thought. He could hear his own breath rasping in the warm air. Memory - which suggested a wooden seat half way along the path - had again proved fallible. The seat had been removed, or perhaps was never there in the first place.

He was pretty desperate by now for somewhere to sit. At the end of the path he crossed onto the grassy banks above the main cricket field, saw the pavilion and then - with relief - the seats, where they'd always been. He reached one of them and sank down. Relieved of the weight upon them, his legs juddered against the wooden slats. The expanse of cricket field was a fuzzy moving image, like something filmed with a hand-held camera. He sat quietly till the dizziness had settled down. He wished he'd taken the opportunity of a good piss back at the main school toilets.

After a bit he began to feel more comfortable - though the prospect of moving from the seat remained intimidating. He lifted his head to take in the surroundings. This had been a favourite spot of his years earlier: a broad expanse of grass rumoured to be the largest cricket ground in the country outside Lords. Around its borders all manner of trees gave a pleasing prospect. The ones immediately opposite marked the farthest extent of the school grounds, beyond which was out of bounds to the boys. He remembered the setting well enough; no surge of memory needed to revive that scene from the past. The incident had been bouncing in and out of his head throughout the day.

It had happened on a warm Sunday evening in summer when, for some reason, about 30 boys had drifted in a crowd to the far side of the cricket ground. He supposed they'd been bored; there were few enough diversions on a school Sabbath. In desperation they'd been talking to three young village lads who'd materialised on the far side of the boundary fence. It was like a scene from L P Hartley's book, The go-between: the chirpy, scruffy village boys and the crowd of young gentlemen, on either side of a fence that divided their worlds. There was some banter, good-natured enough, as far as Rogers could recall. Maybe one of the villagers had said something cheeky and a Mill Hill boy had responded, but nothing untoward. Still, he remembered a village lad saying 'You wait till Uncle 'Arry arrives'.

When he did arrive, along with three more older boys, Uncle Harry was a memorable sight. He had a frame like a blacksmith and a red face with ginger hair sticking up all around it. A wild man. 'So you want to know about village boys, do yer,' he growled, leaping without preamble onto the fence. He stood poised on the top rung looking down at the Mill Hill boys; then he was on them. To be specific, he was on top of Rogers, hitting out with both fists as the pair of them rolled on the ground. Rogers was aware of the man's muscular body against his, and the pin-points of pain as the flailing fists connected with his body and face; aware above all of 30 Mill Hill boys gathered round watching, doing nothing to stop the melee, but for a murmur of dissent as the wild man landed a kick in his ribs - as though the contest was being conducted under the Marquis of Queensbury rules. Strangest of all Rogers, a nervous character who'd always avoided fights, found that being roughed up wasn't half as bad as he'd imagined. He felt almost stimulated by the turn of events. He even found time to notice the other village boys joining in, so that four separate fights were in progress.

Then as quickly as it had begun the whole affair was over; the wild man and friends back across the fence and the Mill Hill boys dispersing to their houses. Rogers didn't see the whole transformation because the ginger-haired bloke was sitting on his face, but it was later ascribed in school mythology to 'the powers of leadership'. At that time they had a head boy called Hinckley-Smith, renowned for dealing sensibly with awkward situations. He fully justified his reputation, first by turning up at the right moment, then by dispersing the scrummage without fuss, reasoning with the village lads and haranguing the Mill Hill contingent. It really was a magical demonstration of natural authority.

Rogers wasn't badly hurt, though he'd sustained a purple scrape down one side of his face. He'd moved well away from the fence to a seat by the pavilion - the same one, in all probability, that was accommodating him 60 years later. A couple of friends had been in attendance, belatedly showing concern for his health. The three of them had lingered there a while as shadows fell across the broad sweep of the cricket ground. In the tranquillity of the evening it had been hard to believe a riot had taken place at all. Then from way beyond the trees on the far side they'd heard it: a raucous voice - Uncle Harry's, no doubt - drifting across the expanse of playing field, far away yet distinct in every word.

'That'll - shake - the - cream - up - in - yer - arses.'

'I beg your pardon.'

It was a man's voice, close to Rogers's ear, and he realised he must have been muttering Uncle Harry's imprecation aloud. But how aloud? How much had the stranger overheard?

'I'm sorry, Rogers said with a little laugh. 'It really wasn't important.'

'Are you all right?' The stranger had moved closer to sit on the end of the seat. He wore a sport jacket with tie, a combination that irresistibly suggested a school connection. His face was intelligent, rather ferrety-looking. 'Forgive me, but you don't look too good,' he said.

'It's all right,' Rogers said. 'I'm just ancient. No cause for alarm.'

'I don't know.' The newcomer was still giving him the once-over. 'Why don't you come into the house here? I can offer you a cup of tea.'

'To Burton Bank?'

'You know it?'

'I was a boy there, a few centuries ago.'

'Well, well,' said the man. 'People often do come back, you know, sit up here taking in the view. I'm Jeremy Clayton, by the way. I'm the BB house master now.'

Rogers wasn't surprised. 'House master, eh! It was Baggy Stanham in my day.'

'Haven't heard the name.'

'Headmaster was Roy Moore. Had a dog called Bruce.' Rogers heard himself gabbling away, but found it hard to stop. 'He used to go on - the head man, that is - about foolhardiness.' He imitated a deep, plummy tone. 'Sheer foolhardiness'.

'Moore? Another blank, I'm afraid.' Clayton was well disposed, but brisk.

'Of course you haven't. They were old even then. Much too old for anyone to remember them now.' Rogers tried to recall some of the younger masters from his time. 'What about Hodgson, Wait, Gallacher?'

Clayton shook his head. 'Must have all gone.'

'Yes, of course. Silly of me.'

'Look,' the ferret-faced chap urged. 'Do come in for a cup of tea. Something stronger, if you like.'

'Nice of you,' said Rogers, and it was nice - the hand of courtesy extended to the Mill Hill brotherhood through the ages. 'But honestly, I'd rather sit here. Feels very peaceful actually.'

Clayton stood reluctantly, shook hands, and strode off towards the house. The old man was left alone on the bank, gazing at the sunlit cricket field. Rogers was feeling peaceful all right - he'd meant what he said - but immobile too. It was as if all the energy had drained from his body through sleeves and other apertures in clothing. His thoughts were meandering way, way back. He was at home, preparing to leave for another school term, while his mother sat in the armchair sewing name tags onto new clothing. 'Michael Rogers 196BB.'

He drifted into a doze, head nodding, then jerked awake. Someone standing nearby might just have heard him muttering, in his decidedly middle-class voice.

'Shake the cream up in yer arses.'

Printed in Great Britain
by Amazon